'X Y, Z'

.

Jess Molyneux

Cover Illustration: Danielle Furness

DEDICATION

To the real Jay and Alex: I love you, you're the
reason I do anything... now for pity's sake,
put this book down and don't read this pile of
filth your mother's written.

M, you're amazing. Thank you isn't anywhere
near enough, but it's all I've got. ILY.

ACKNOWLEDGEMENTS

There are so many people whom I should mention, I apologise if I miss you out...

Sally-Anne Tapia Bowes, for telling me I was born to write and making me a bit jealous when she published her book.

My proof reading crew: Caz Abbatt, Michelle Lowe, Sarah Stewart and Paula McKinney. The positive feedback was hugely appreciated. Special mention to Teresita.

My wonderful mother (who **is** obsessed with shopping channels, but is otherwise very different from Zoe's mum), sister and brother who have had to listen to me go on about this book since I began. Hope I don't embarrass you.

My oldest (in terms of how long I've known them, not age!) friends Lorena Rivas and Sarah Davis, for always believing in me.

Mr Joseph Hartley. Without his encouragement, I would never have started writing at all.

Tess Malpus and Mel Swift, who have never been my driving instructor or auntie, but have been fantastic friends.

i

CHAPTER 1

'And this', Mr Burton continued, 'will be the most crucial year of your lives. This is your final year of secondary school education. You came into this year as students, but will leave as young adults.'

Yeah yeah... it's September 7th, we're at the start of Year 13 and we're getting the same lecture that the head has trotted out to Sixth Formers in Friday assemblies for the last five years.

He doesn't have to tell me. I know this is an important year all right, but not for the reason he means. I work hard, I'm on course to get the grades I need for uni. I'm actually not really worried about that. For me, school work is just logical. Put the effort in, and the results will come. My problem is a bit more... hard to control than that.

I'm sick of being alone. I don't want to think of myself as one of those sappy women I read about in my mum's magazines who drift from loser to loser because they can't function without a man in their lives, but a bit of attention would be nice. I get on okay with lads, but I guess they tend to just see me as the brainy girl to beg for help with their assignment the day before it's due in.

It didn't bother me too much when I was younger. Going to an all-girls school, boys seemed to be more like another species than the opposite sex and I supposed I just never missed what I never had... but during the last year of being in the Sixth Form, which is merged with the boys' school down the road, I've definitely been feeling like something's missing. A big, boyfriend-shaped gap in my life.

I wish I knew why the boys at school hardly ever ask me out. I mean, I know I'm no supermodel, but I'm not that bad, am I? Do I give off some horrible, 'Do not approach this weirdo under any circumstances' vibe or something? My best mate, Kate, has had the same boyfriend since Year 11 – and while he doesn't do it for me (that's one of the greatest things about Kate, we'll definitely never fight over a man, something we've known since discussing our Year 8 celebrity crushes and finding we liked totally different types), I can't help but feel a bit jealous of what she's got.

I have had the odd boy ask me out in the last couple of years, but never anything serious. We never seemed to get past a few dates, going to the cinema or bowling... then either he'd lose interest or I would.

I know it's silly. I've been brought up to not see having a man as the be-all-and-end-all. Since my parents broke up when I was eight, my Mum's really tried to instil it into me that I should be never be dependent on a man, and she's red hot on the 'It's your body and you should never feel pressured into anything you don't want to do' message.

And I totally agree, but... what if I *do* want to? What if I feel left out, like everyone else is being chosen and I'm being left behind? I feel like everyone else has got someone and I'm the only loser left, desperate and dateless. I'm nearly eighteen and I've never had more than some rather crap snogs with boys I'd rather forget.

I just know that if I had someone, someone who was mine, life would be a thousand times better. And then there's, you know... sex. I know Kate's done it. I overhear other girls at school talk about times they've done it. I'm starting to think I'm just terminally undesirable and I should become a nun.

Huh. Not sure anyone would notice.

But how do I make it happen? If this was an assignment, I could research around the problem, read up on it, work harder 'til I cracked it... but getting a boy to really like me is the one thing that seems to be out of my control. Sometimes it feels like everyone in the world's got someone, except lonely loser me.

"Oh Zo, don't panic about it. You're gorgeous," Kate says to me in the common room over one of our daily chats, where we have a coffee, moan about school and (in my case, not hers) the unending dating dry patch.

"If anything, I bet that's why you're single. All the mings in our school don't approach you 'cause they know you're out of their league."

I let out a laugh. "Well, that's okay! Have you seen the state of most of the lads at our school? You're lucky you got Danny from St Anthony's", I say, actually truthfully. While I'm never going to fancy Danny, he does make Kate happy, so I guess he's alright. "Although, well, maybe one of them's not too bad."

"What? You like someone?" Kate puts down her cup and looks straight at me, eyes interrogating me for the juicy details. "Don't say you don't, I can tell when you're lying. Who is he?"

I can feel my cheeks turning pink and my mouth twitching upwards involuntarily. "Well, yeah, there is someone. He's in my English class, so you won't know him. He's alright."

Alright. We all know what *that* means. I'm pretty much obsessed.

Alex Ryan. The one thing that makes sitting through four hours of A Level English Literature each week bearable. He's doing English and Theatre Studies because he's going to be an actor. He already is one, you could say; he's done a few small TV parts, including a bit-part on our local soap for a week last year that had all the Year 9 girls chasing after him. Well, move over, little girls. This one's mine... or at least, I wish he was.

If the boys aren't approaching me, maybe it's time I started being, well, a bit more proactive.

I first saw him at the start of Year 12 when we

both found ourselves in Miss Dey's English class. I wasn't sure about him at first. As he talked about his ambitions and the couple of acting jobs he'd already done, I thought he'd be a bit big-headed and annoying. He's not though. Once I got talking to him, he was really nice. He didn't think he was better than the rest of us even though he'd been on telly; he'd get his assignments in on time, lend me a pen or, more often, borrow one from me and well, just act normal really.

I've spoken to him loads of times before, but never anything very deep because, if I'm honest, I've always been too in awe of him. I've always thought someone as gorgeous as him would never even look at me... but after a whole year of not venturing further than small talk in the common room in case I made a div of myself in front of him, and pairing up with him to make notes in English (slightly more comfortable; at least with the subject of literature I could speak with a bit more confidence), I reckon if I don't at least try to get to know him better, I'm going to regret it forever.

I guess I really fell for him when he had a part in the chorus at the local pantomime last Christmas. I borrowed my six year old cousin so I had an excuse to see it, and then just spent the whole time gazing at Alex, who managed to look fit even in one of those generic panto chorus outfits of colourful dungarees and those shoes with the massive buckles on them; if you can do that, you're obviously pretty damn hot.

Then, my confidence got a bit of a boost when Sasha McCormack, the self-appointed popular princess of our year group (why is the 'popular' girl at school always someone you bloody hate?) assumed she could just have him... and Alex wasn't interested! Princess Sasha actually getting the knock-back was the talk of the common room that week. I'm not sure why she even went after him: she usually goes for big muscly types and Alex is slim, cute rather than hunky and, well, not one of the meat-headed footy lads she usually goes for. I reckon the fact that she chased after him the week he'd been on the telly had a lot to do with it.

Still, it was him turning her down that made me a) love him even more for not being interested in that skank, and b) think I had maybe a better than average chance, because as a short, clever brunette, I'm the total opposite of that blonde Poundshop WAG, and if he doesn't like her... I could be deluding myself but, over the last eight months since then, him not liking her has eventually spiralled in my mind into a definite indication that he might just go for a girl like me.

It's been a whole year since I've met him and I've never told a soul about how I feel, not even Kate. Until today.

I mean, imagine if I told him I like him and he just laughed in my face? Or even if he just turned me down without being nasty, I think I'd have to change A levels – no, make that change schools – rather than have to keep facing him.

He's just perfect. I don't know whether it's the huge brown eyes, the soft, fine dark brown hair that falls across his forehead or the way he wears *anything* – trust me, this boy could look amazing in a bin bag, so couple that with seriously fit dress sense – but, I'm telling you, everything about him is totally fuckable.

And I would do it with him. Definitely.

If I'm being totally honest, I guess I've been secretly in love with him for the whole of Year 12. I haven't told anyone about how I feel because, well, I'm not sure I could even trust Kate not to laugh and tell me I'm punching above my weight, big time. He's gorgeous, funny and talented and I'm, well, I'm me... still, he does seem to get on okay with me, and not just because he wants help with his essays. Maybe, just maybe, he might like me?

I've had enough of being a lonely little virgin, so I've made up my mind to give it a shot... and by that, I mean all or nothing. Tonight, he's either coming home with me or I'm going to enrol at the ropey Sixth Form college on the other side of town on Monday. It can't be worse than the months of dreaming about him and wishing he knew about the major crush I've had on him all year.

I know I must sound like a bit of a desperate slag, telling you what I'm planning: to bring him home and lose my virginity when I'm not even going out with him. But he's not some stranger, is he? I've known him a whole year. I know it sounds wrong, but even if he dumped me afterwards, at least I'd have had him, even if it was only once. I can't think of anyone I'd want more for my first time, and I want my first time to be tonight.

It's my mate Jay's 18th tonight, and he's thrown an open invitation to pretty much everyone in the year. If Kate's my best girlfriend, Jay's definitely my best male mate. He used to live in the same road as me so we used to play together as little kids, and as we got older, we'd walk to our schools together – him to the boys' one, me to the girls'.

Jay moved away when his parents won £10.8m on the lottery when we were in Year 9, but he hasn't changed a bit. We've always just hung out as we did before, only now he's got a bigger bedroom than me. And a swimming pool.

He's 6ft and blond with a solid, muscular frame. Not my type, but Kate was definitely keen when she first met him. I had to explain she'll never be his type – that'd be more like Connor, his boyfriend.

Anyway, his parents have hired a function room in town, so even beside what I'm hoping will happen between me and Alex, it should be the party of the year. I'm going to try to approach Alex and at least I'll know whether he likes me or not. Then, I can either bring him home and get rid of the virgin curse, or come home alone and sob into my pillow – but at least I'll know.

There is one thing I do wonder about: considering he's so fit, as far as I can make out, Alex hasn't gone out with any of the girls at school. Surely he could have anyone he wanted, so why hasn't he?

I know what you could be thinking at this point, because I have thought of it as well. Of course it's occurred to me that even if Alex likes me as a person, I could be heading for the Gay Best Friendzone. Luckily, Jay's already made a few enquiries on that front and can confirm that Alex is definitely a ladies man.

All I have to do now is get him to come home with me.

The timing couldn't be better. I live with my mum, who's an A&E nurse. When I got old enough to be left on my own a couple of years ago, she started doing some night shifts. So far I've only used the time on my own for some pretty dreadful hairbrush karaoke, boxset marathons and trying in vain to follow makeup tutorials on YouTube, but tonight I'll have the place to myself again while Mum's at work... only maybe this time I won't be alone.

Mum's not too old or stiff, and she's seen enough young people come to A&E on a Friday night to know what some kids get up to, so I don't think she'd hit the roof if she knew I'd brought a boy back. I think I'd just like my first time to be just me and him, without wondering if my mother was awake in the room next door.

Just me and Alex. Even thinking about it makes me smile. In my mind, I imagine how

it'll be, all in soft focus and slow-motion.
Tender, romantic and perfect, like in a film.
The plan is this: get close to Alex, make sure
I'm on the same bus home as him, then get
him to come home with me, somehow,
anyhow... and then it'll happen.

Unless it doesn't, but let's not think about
that just now, eh?

I never usually spend too long deciding what
to wear for a night out, but I've got to get
everything right tonight. I'm going to
remember this night for the rest of my life, or
if it all goes wrong, at least I can remember I
looked good at the start of it all...

I can't believe I left it 'til the day of the party to
pick an outfit. I thought wearing something I
feel comfortable in might be a good idea, but I
chickened out at the last minute and decided
I'd feel a bit better in something new.

Straight after school I head into town, and
after a few hours wandering round the shops,
I end up going with a fab red and black 50s
style dress. Red applique satin roses on a
black netted skirt, bodice just low cut enough.
It'll go perfectly with a pair of Iron Fist shoes
I've only worn once. I send Kate a picture of
the dress from the shop changing room before

I go and pay for it. After a couple of minutes, I get the reply: "Love it! Have you picked your underwear yet?"

Underwear? I hadn't even thought about that! Of course I'll need new underwear. Right now, the contents of my knicker drawer tend to be Primark or supermarket bras and multipacks of basic white knickers. Not exactly spanking, pristine new ones either, if I'm going to be totally honest. We've all got knickers we'd refer to as 'period pants' – well, let's just say most of mine date from the Jurassic Period. I'm just not that interested in my knickers, and let's face it, no-one else has ever been either, really.

The only other ones I've got are a set Mum got me last Christmas. They're pink jersey, with a teddy hugging a heart on them – err, no. That doesn't exactly scream 'Sex Goddess' does it?

So I head to the lingerie department and start looking. I feel a bit lost. I wish Kate was here to help me. I know why she thought of it immediately, she's always treating herself (or is it Danny?) to lacy, silky matching sets when we go shopping, but I'm not actually a big fan of fancy underwear. No-one ever sees it. If I'm going to spend that amount of money, I'd rather have a new pair of shoes, or a handbag that at least people will notice without me having to strip off.

After sending pics of a few possible candidates to her, Kate eventually helps me decide on a lilac set, mostly satin but with a bit of lace around the bra cups and a panel in the front of the knickers. I did consider going padded for a second or two, but if he's that much of a boob man, he'll be in a for a disappointment when the bra comes off and he's left with my 34Bs. No, he can take me as I am, or not at all.

I feel a wave of worry mixed with excitement as I leave the lingerie department clutching my tiny little bag. I just hope the things I've picked will be good enough. They're not the fanciest or most expensive, but I'm a student so I can't shell out that much, and I doubt I'll wear them again, especially if they don't have the desired effect. They're a bit uncomfortable compared with my usual jersey pants. He'd better appreciate this.

It's 8.30pm now, Kate's in my room and we're both getting ready. I look at myself in my full length mirror: underwear on, dress swishing at knee level, and my hair's shiny and straight. Perfect. Just need Kate to do my makeup and it's game on. I either get my man or – well, I'll just be single like I was before. No big deal. Nothing to get upset about.

Yeah, right.

We arrive at the venue at about 9.15. I've already had a few drinks while we were getting dressed to get warmed up, even though there's a free bar. Even in my new dress, I'm not confident enough to launch my attack on nothing but Diet Coke and orange juice. I find Jay, who's been there since the beginning greeting his guests, have a chat to him about how his birthday's been, and jokingly (not that jokingly if I'm honest) ask about having a go sometime in the two-year-old Ford Focus his parents have given him as a present.

Ron, Jay's dad, laughs. "You'll be able to take this one somewhere nice now, eh Jason?"

I smile weakly. Jay's parents always seem convinced we're a couple. I don't know how or when he's going to tell them the truth. Still, that's Jay's decision to make. I just go for the option of not contradicting him or Ang when they say things like, "Homework... I hope that's all you're doing!" with an exaggerated wink when Jay and I go upstairs at his house. I'm not sure why they want him to be with me so much. Maybe it's just the idea of someone who knew him before he had money.

About fifteen minutes later, Alex arrives.

I'm going to find it very hard to be cool

because he looks gorgeous on an average Wednesday in the canteen, but tonight... wow, he's next-level hot. He's got a subtle hint of eyeliner emphasising those massive brown eyes, and (it couldn't be any more perfect) he's wearing a sexy black suit, white shirt open at the collar and not tucked in, a black tie done loosely so the knot's hanging down and a red flower. On anyone else it could look contrived; it takes the charisma of Alex Ryan to carry it off.

"Well, he's a bit pretty for me, but I can see why you like him," Kate grins. "I'll see you on the bus later; don't come back 'til you've got him. Go for it!"

When I walk over and stand by him, wearing the same colours, we fit together. It's like he knows. One or two people have already pointed out how our outfits complement each other. Some people are saying, "Oh, they're like a couple," and other similar things.

Somewhere in the background, I hear Sasha mutter, "Pair of freaks," but who cares what that jealous bitch thinks?

Alex comes closer to me, looks me up and down and smiles. "Hey. I guess this means we've got to dance together since we've come as a matching pair." I'm not arguing, in fact I doubt I could say anything as he takes my hand and leads me towards the dancefloor.

For the rest of the night, Alex belongs to me. We dance together, we drink together, we talk together. I'm an average dancer at best, but Drama student Alex knows exactly how to move me around the dancefloor... bodes well for later, I can't help but think to myself. After a while, we take a break and sit down.

"I'm so glad you came tonight," he says. "Look, can I talk to you about something?"

"Yeah, of course."

I don't like this. Why is he going all serious on me? We've been having a laugh up to this point. Oh, I know what's coming next. He's going to say he knows I like him, and like the sweetie he is, he's going to let me down gently.

Oh well, it was a nice fantasy while it lasted. I can see tonight ending with a massive box of tissues and then having to find ways to avoid him for the rest of the year. And then I'm going to burn this itchy bra. It's been doing my head in all night.

"Look, Zoe, I..." he takes a sip of his drink. Why is he acting all strange? We've been more comfortable together tonight than we've ever been. Or at least, I thought we were.

He takes a deep breath. Is he nervous or something?

"I was never sure how to talk to you at school, so I just stuck to silly things like borrowing pens. The thing is, well, I've liked you for ages, but I was never sure you'd feel the same. And to be honest, for most of last year, I thought you were with Jay."

What? Is this for real? He didn't know how to approach me? He's the super-confident, hottest boy in the year... and he wasn't sure he could have me? I mean, me?

1 am. The party was great, but now everyone is on the coach home, laid on by Jay's parents. The atmosphere's noisy but good natured and I'm in a vague alcoholic haze, but I know what I'm doing... I know what I want. Alex and I still haven't even kissed yet, in fact we haven't done anything since he said he liked me. Right then, that moment would have been the perfect time to kiss, but then the music stopped and we had to gather at the stage while Jay's older brother made the obligatory 18th birthday speech, complete with slideshow of embarrassing photos.

To cool everyone down at the end of a night of dancing in a hot room, they were handing out Calippos as people left. Every time Alex catches my eye, I give mine a playful lick and a meaningful smile. He gets it. He's got to come home with me now: he said he likes me, he can't possibly not realise I like him, and even if I do say it myself, my tongue-game is pretty strong.

Jay's parents seem to be giving each other concerned looks. I've obviously not acted much like their son's girlfriend tonight, but I've never lied to them. I just hope Jay doesn't face any questions he's not ready for later.

People are taking selfies, mostly involving Calippos in suspect poses, a bit of singing's broken out at the back of the bus and everyone seems happy. I need to talk to Alex again, though. Now I know he likes me, I can't just end tonight without even getting to kiss him. I move across the aisle and sit next to him, just as Kate points her phone at us. He turns on his gorgeous smile, and I've got a mile-wide grin on my face. Then, seemingly out of nowhere, he turns to me, looks me in the eyes and says, 'You look amazing tonight.'

I wish I could say something back to him, but I'm too busy trying to stem the tidal wave about to break in my knickers to speak... then he kisses me. A cry of 'Whoooa!' goes up around the coach. I'd have preferred my first kiss with him to be a little more private and a bit less like when someone drops a plate in the canteen, but it's still electrifying. I feel my nipples tingle as his tongue reaches in to part my lips. I don't care who's looking. I want him. Now.

The coach pulls in. "You getting off here?" I ask him.

"I am now," he says. "I'll make sure you're okay, see you to your door."

I say goodbye to Kate, who simply grins and whispers, "Well played, girl. Now, take him home, shag him senseless and remember: I want to know everything tomorrow!"

As we walk the few roads to my house, we talk about what a great night it's been and who's going to be embarrassed on Instagram tomorrow... then when we get to my door, I hesitate. I can't ask him in for a coffee, that'd sound so stupid... ask him in for a shag and I'll just sound desperate. Okay, I *am* desperate, but he doesn't have to know that, does he? And anyway, imagine that getting round school on Monday? I might be dying to do it, but I don't want the whole world knowing about it.

In the end, aware I haven't said anything and we've hovered on my step for two minutes, I end up saying, 'Well, erm, do you want to come in... for something?'

In the house, I invite him to sit down and take off my jacket. Away from the party and our audience, all my earlier 'I'm gonna have him tonight' bravado has deserted me and I'm bricking it at the thought that this might actually happen. He's on the couch, so where do I sit? On the chair opposite? This isn't a bloody job interview. Is right next to him too obvious? He seems to know what I'm thinking, because he pats the cushion next to him, gives me that knicker-soaking smile again and says, 'Here'.

I sit down next to him, and his arm falls round my shoulder. He looks me right in the eyes and I know we're going to kiss again. This time, we keep going in a series of lovely long kisses as he starts to explore my mouth with his tongue.

I pull away a little in surprise as I reach across to hold him and my hand brushes across the hardness of his groin. He's up for this, for sure. Well, if I don't want to be a terrified little virgin for the rest of my life, I'm going to have to go for it. Now.

I start running my hand up and down his erection, all the time looking him straight in the eye. His eyes narrow with pleasure and he says softly, "Oh babe, keep going. That's beautiful." He slips his hand into my bra and starts caressing my left nipple.

"This is nice," he says, stroking one of the satin cups.

I bloody love this bra. In fact, I'm going back tomorrow and getting six more so I can wear it every day.

After a couple of minutes, he eases me off the couch and we're both lying on the living room floor. I lie on my back and he straddles me. Man, even through his trousers I can feel how hard he is. And how big. Is that really going to fit inside me? Can I really do this?

He pauses for a second and says, "Zoe, I don't want to stop. Are you okay with it if I carry on?"

All I can manage is a nervous, "Yeah... yeah, I want to."

This is it. It's going to happen. I feel suddenly self-conscious about how damp my knickers are, but as he slips in a finger either side and moves them down gently, he doesn't seem to mind.

By now I'm a mixture of tingling with anticipation and absolutely petrified. He gets off me for a second, turns on his side and takes a condom out of his jacket pocket. It takes him a few seconds to slide it on. How many times has he done this, I wonder? Still, I'm just glad he did because I'd never have known how to bring it up – at what point can you say, 'Hold on a minute, could you just pop that dick in a plastic bag before we go any further?' I bought some, but they're upstairs in my knicker drawer.

He returns to his position on top of me and whispers, "It's okay, just relax. I'll be gentle."

My cheeks burn. He knows. He knows this is my first time. So much for my cocky, confident woman of the world act I've been keeping up all evening.

As he guides himself inside, I let out a gasp and he kisses me. "You'll be fine, come on." Then he starts thrusting his hips up and down, slowly at first but getting quicker as his breath becomes shorter. I'm too terrified to move, if I'm honest.

After what seems like only about two minutes, his whole body stiffens, he lets out a groan, and I guess that's it. My first time is over. I'd built it up in my head that it'd be some magical, romantic experience and it turned out to be a five-minute-fuck on the living room carpet. I didn't even take my dress off. I've been such an idiot.

For a brief moment, I feel tears welling up at the sides of my eyes, but then he looks at me again and gives me a gentle kiss on the lips.

"Hey, are you okay? Sorry about that, I was just so horny I went off in a minute. Tell you what, you can pretend you actually did ask me in for coffee and we'll wait for a bit," he says, between soft, warm kisses, "and then I'll take you up to bed and make love to you."

What a pile of shite, I think. He doesn't love me, he's just saying that because he wants another go and he can sense I'm disappointed. However, while my brain knows it's bullshit, the rest of me has totally bought it. I'm quivering uncontrollably and I can't speak. Oh, he's good, I'll give him that.

In fact, right now, I'm willing to give him anything he wants.

CHAPTER 2

A crack of sunlight between my curtains wakes me up. I often wake up early at the weekends, and for a second, I just lie still, looking forward to my usual Saturday extra time in bed. Then the events of last night flash into my mind and I look across to the other side of my bed.

He's still here.

He's asleep, and looking every bit as perfect as last night, even with slightly smudged eyeliner and morning hair. I think back to last night, and then my mind starts editing and deciding which bits I'm going to tell Kate about first: definitely how he led me up the stairs, holding my hand, not so much when he stopped at the top of the stairs because he didn't know which was my room, and while he was standing there, his trousers fell down – well, he didn't bother doing them up as we moved from the living room! I just thought, this doesn't happen in the films... but the rest of it was the magic, amazing, best-night-of-my-life stuff I'd imagined it'd be.

From standing, arms wrapped around each other as we kissed, he moved me gently towards the bed, where we sat for a second before realising we should just get to the point and lie down. We peeled each other's clothes off, throwing them to the floor while we locked arms, legs, lips... then he lay me on my back, leaned over me and said, "Let's get you ready for round two." I started to pucker my lips up for a kiss, but he started moving back from me and down towards the other end of the bed. I just thought, where the hell are you going?

Oh. I see.

His tongue sent waves of ecstasy through me that I had no idea I could feel. Let's just say that after a couple of minutes of his gentle but persistent lapping, I was more than ready. Seems I'm not the only one with good tongue-game.

But you know what? I think I'll just tell Kate he's a good kisser.

I come back to the present and look around my room. His clothes are scattered over the floor, but I can see I did at least drape my dress over a chair afterwards. Suddenly, I feel painfully aware of the fact that we're both naked. I reach to the floor at the side of my bed to grab my nightie, and try to put it on. I'm quiet, but the movement still wakes him up.

"Hey", he says, a little groggy. "Don't bother with that, I think we've both seen pretty much everything now. Come here and give me a hug."

I drop the nightie and slide myself under his arm, with my arm across his chest. I'm not saying anything, but inside my head I'm shouting, 'Oh my God! I'm in bed with Alex Ryan!' on a loop.

Realising I can't stay silent forever, I eventually come up with, "Well, that was a good night, wasn't it? Jay's party, I mean."

What am I saying? Does losing your virginity turn you into a total idiot? Why am I talking such rubbish? I've just spent the night in bed with this boy, and now I can't even have a conversation with him. Perhaps I should just shut up.

"Yeah, the party was great," he says, "but well,

it wasn't the best bit, was it?" He leans in and gives me a kiss. We both keep our lips together. He may be gorgeous, but I guess even Alex Ryan gets morning bad breath. I don't care. He's perfect to me and he's here. That's all that matters.

I make coffees and bring them up, and we sit in bed drinking, kissing and just being close to each other. I'll have to kick him out in a couple of hours because Mum usually comes back around lunchtime, but right now I don't want this to end. Ever.

At eleven o'clock, Alex pulls his clothes back on and leaves. Before he goes, he gives me one last lingering kiss. "That was a great night. I'll see you Monday, yeah?"

I shut the door after him and, when I've seen him turn the corner of my road, I jump up and down for a few seconds and scream with delight.

I got him! I only bloody got him!

Right, time to get in the shower and scrub the smell of him off me before Mum comes back.

After my shower, I get dressed, and that's when reality hits me. You know how in the film 'Big', Tom Hanks' character has had a night of passion and then he walks into work with a confident swagger and a massive grin on his face?

Well, the reality is nothing like that.

I'm sore as hell. One thing they don't tell you about doing it for the first time is how much it actually hurts. Thinking about it, I suppose I shouldn't be too surprised. Nothing bigger than a tampon (and okay, maybe one time I experimented with a plastic toothbrush case from Superdrug, but I haven't even told Kate that) has ever gone up there, so no wonder I'm aching with every step today. When I picked up the condom with a tissue and put it in a carrier bag (I didn't want Mum spotting it in the bin) there were streaks of blood on the outside – so much for that magazine article I read a few years back that said the hymen can get broken by playing bloody netball! I feel like a lot of the things I've been told about sex might just be a load of nonsense.

Also, I feel like Mum's going to know, like there's a big neon sign over my head saying, 'She's done it!'. There doesn't seem to be, though. Mum just comes in at around midday, asks if I had a nice time at the party, puts the kettle on and starts making a shopping list.

"Tell you what, Mum," I say, hoping my voice doesn't sound wobbly. "I'll pick up the shopping for you. I'm going out to meet Kate now but I'll get it on the way back. Be back around five, okay? See you later."

Everything's crazy. On the surface, I'm still her daughter, nipping down to the shops and letting her know what time I'll be back, but in my head I've changed. I'm not a kid anymore. On the way out, I look at myself in the hall mirror, to see if I look any different. I don't see any new maturity or loved-up glow, just a massive spot emerging on the side of my nose. Fucking great. How long's that been there?

Right. I may not have had a serious boyfriend before, but I know the rules. Don't go calling him up the same day, or even the next day. The last thing I want to do is scare him off by coming across as an obsessed nutter... but I can't stop thinking about when I'll see him again! I mean, we weren't even going out and we did it! It just seemed so right at the time, and it's not as though I'd just met him or anything, but it suddenly dawns on me that I don't know much about him beyond our small talk in lessons and only-slightly-bigger talk at the party.

I spent the whole weekend wondering, what if he doesn't call, and then just blanks me on

Monday? I know what I said before, but I'll feel like such an idiot if I've gone and had sex with him, thinking he's The One, but all he wanted to do was use me because I was there and he could smell the desperation.

So now it's Monday break, and if I thought I had to put some effort into picking my outfit for Friday night, that was nothing compared with today. Our school doesn't have uniform for Sixth Formers, just an 'appropriate dress code', so as long as we don't take the piss (like the time one of Sasha's stupid mates took the 'any top and black skirt/trousers' rule to its extreme and showed up in a bikini top and skirt that showed her knickers and nearly caused Mr Burton to impose the same uniform as the Year 7s on us) we can wear what we want.

I end up going with a pair of black Capri pants and a white top with red polka dots. If all eyes are going to be on Alex Ryan's Possible New Girlfriend, I've got to look my best.

I've got English after break and I'm waiting in the part of the school canteen that's done out like a café area and only available to Sixth Formers. Kate and Jay are out on a Science trip today so I'm alone, sipping my coffee and trying not to look like I'm watching Alex on the other side of the room. He's with his mates, less dressed up than the other night in a white t-shirt with a check shirt over it, undone. I hear a big laugh from the group and just hope it's not because he's told them about the girl he went and shagged on her living room floor and who he's got no intention of calling again, or (please God no) the teddy I've still got – at least it sits on my window sill, not on my bed.

He doesn't even sit next to me in the lesson. This is not good. Then, just to make it totally perfect, Miss Dey chooses him and me to read parts in the play we're studying: 'Much Ado About Nothing.' I'm Beatrice and he's Benedick, two characters who everyone can see fancy the pants off each other. The only people who can't see it is them. Nice one, Miss. I swear teachers can be evil sometimes.

At the end of the lesson, it's lunchtime. I usually stay in school and catch up with Kate, but since she's not here today I might go and hide in the local library, the only way we're allowed out of school during the day. I don't really want to risk seeing Alex anymore. Then, just as I'm picking up my ring-binder, he comes over to me.

"Hi. Just wanted to see how you are after the other night," he says quietly.

"Oh, you remember about that, do you?" I say, unable to stop myself sounding annoyed.

That was stupid of me. What do I want him to do? Stick to my side at all times, follow me into the toilets? I look at him and give him an apologetic smile.

"I'm sorry, Alex. When you didn't come over to me at break, I thought you were blanking me and you weren't going to talk to me anymore."

"Oh no, it wasn't like that, sorry. I just didn't want you to think I was stalking you, and yeah, I did want to tell my mates about getting off with you. Why wouldn't I?"

He smiles at me as he says,

"Don't worry, I didn't go telling them everything. Look, do you fancy getting some lunch now, and maybe come round to mine to work on that assignment Miss just gave us tonight?"

I feel reassured. It wasn't just a one night thing. He likes me. My smile gives him the answer.

After lunch, I head back to lessons. Is it a bit wrong of me that I was disappointed no-one seemed to be staring at us? I wanted to shout, 'Excuse me! Fairly average girl with fittest boy in Sixth Form over here!', but the only person who seemed to notice was Miss Dey, who sat across the canteen with her baked potato and a look that said, 'Ha! I knew it!'

CHAPTER 3

Alex's house is about ten minutes' walk from
mine, in a reasonably nice road. His parents'
cars are on the drive, so I guess it really will
be a night of doing homework. He answers the
door and shows me into the long, knocked-
through living and dining room. At the back,
Alex's mum is sitting at a table, applying
makeup. Quite a lot of makeup. She looks a
bit fearsome, If I'm honest. I just look at her,
say nothing and she carries on as if I'm not
there.

A minute later, a tall man of about fifty comes
downstairs and into the room, filing it with a
strong smell of aftershave. "You ready yet,
love? We don't want all the parking spots to
go, do we?" before noticing me, then turning to
Alex and asking, "Aren't you going to
introduce us, son? Don't leave the poor girl

standing there like a lemon."

Alex is much quieter at home, a lot different to his confident persona at school. It's quite strange to watch. "Erm, this is my mum and dad. This is Zoe."

His mother zips up the makeup bag, gets up from the table and says, "Nice to meet you, Zoe," before going out into the hallway. As she goes, she gives her husband a smile and a raised eyebrow. What does that mean? Does she think I'm some man-eating little tramp, chasing after her son, or does that look mean I'm the latest in a very long line?

I smile shyly, give an almost inaudible hello, then listen while they give Alex some instructions about making sure his brother goes to bed on time. Then they leave. I look at Alex, whose face seems to be saying, 'Surprise!'

Oh well, maybe the homework can wait. I've got a free period tomorrow.

As soon as their car's off the drive, Alex pulls me down onto the couch and kisses me several times.

"I've been wanting to do that all day," he says. As he leans in for another, I'm a bit nervous.

"What about your brother? What if he comes down and sees us?"

"He won't. I told him he could play on my Xbox in my room if he just didn't come down. Don't worry. He's nine years old and he's got a drink up there. He'll be fine."

All the same, with him upstairs we know sex is definitely out of the question, something I'm a bit relieved about actually because I'm still a little sore. Instead, we spend the evening kissing, talking and watching telly. I suppose you could say it's our first actual date.

An hour or so later, once Alex has gone up and checked that Leo's asleep, the kissing gets a bit more adventurous. Long, slow kisses, with his tongue venturing into my mouth. I'm not really sure what to do, so I respond in the same way, moving it around a little. It feels weird, and not very sexy really. I thought the French were supposed to be experts on this sort of thing? As far as I can see, it just seems to be something to do when your little brother's asleep upstairs so you can't shag, but you're gagging to poke some part of your body into your girlfriend.

Am I even his girlfriend though? Okay, he didn't blank me after Friday night and we're here now, but what's the official definition? I certainly wasn't introduced to his parents with, 'This is Zoe, my girlfriend,' was I? I suppose this is what I get for being too afraid to talk to him for a whole year, then jumping his bones the minute he showed me the slightest bit of interest.

He pulls away from my face, then undoes three of the buttons on my top.

"Alex, what are you doing?" It was all very well the other night at my house, when I knew no-one could come in until morning, but I feel a lot more self-conscious at his place.

"Don't worry. Leo sleeps like a stone and Mum and Dad are at the theatre. Plays don't end 'til about ten o'clock so we've got ages yet."

Oh well, if you put it like that... I lie back against a cushion while he licks his middle fingers on each hand, then reaches inside my bra and starts running them in little circles around each nipple. He looks at me and grins.

"Oh you like that, don't you?"

They are, as my dad used to say, like football studs. We used to watch some show on kids' TV when I was little and he always referred to one of the presenters as 'Football Studs' when speaking to my mum because you could see her nips through her top. In fact, I think I read years later that the makers of the show did it on purpose to appease the bored dads watching with their kids. I never understood what he meant until years after, but I sure as hell get it now.

I do the same for him, not sure whether it'd have the same effect on a boy. Maybe it does, because after a few minutes he moves my hand towards where he's got another massive hard-on.

"Feel that, babe," he whispers.

I start stroking it gently, as I did the other night – but what else can I do? We can't do IT, can we? I know he said his brother's asleep, but kids wake up all the time. I don't want him coming down and seeing his big brother, his role-model and hero for all I know, banging some random girl on the couch! Actually, to tell the truth I'm not really bothered about some kid I've never met, more the shame of getting caught.

It does feel good, though. I carry on stroking, my fingers brushing against his jeans, enjoying the thought that he's so turned on. The he breaks the silence.

"Will you go down on me? Come on, it'll be okay, they won't be back for a while yet."

Oh fuck. Despite my Calippo-based flirting on the bus the other night, I've never done anything like this before. I've read all the usual magazine 'How To..' articles, but to be honest, pretty much the only thing I know is the golden rule: that it might be called a blow job, but you don't blow. I wonder why they did that? Maybe they thought 'suck job' sounded a bit... well, sucky.

As for anything else you should do, I'm a bit clueless. I curse myself for making lolly-licking promises I'm not sure I can keep as I unzip his jeans and it pops out of the slit in his boxer shorts like a fleshy Jack-in-the-box. Arrgh!

Alex Ryan is the fittest lad in the world. Face, body and personality. He's like the one time God got it completely right... but I can only assume God had turned up for work with a bit of a hangover the day he did his penis. It's ugly as sin. I hope all men's bits are this unattractive, and I haven't just got a particularly bad one.

I begin by sliding my hands up and down. It feels weird. Then I know I can't put it off any longer and I kneel down close to him, and take him in my mouth. I have to really open my jaws up to get it in, and then I start sucking.

It may be about the size and thickness of a Calippo, but refreshing and fruit-flavoured it is not. I can't say I'm enjoying this much at all. The whole thing must have been invented by a man, 'cause it quite literally sucks.

"Not so hard," he says. "just gently. And move your mouth back and forward on it."

Again, I feel a bit needled that this is obviously not his first time if he can be so specific about what he wants, but as I take his advice, it does get better. The saliva created by moving my mouth forms a kind of lube-barrier, which does at least take some of the taste away.

"That's it, keep going," he says breathily. "Won't be long now."

For a second I'm pleased that I got there in the end, but that's replaced by the sharp realisation that 'Won't be long now' means he's not far from finishing, and that the current location of his dick is in my bloody mouth! Oh shit, what do I do? What if I try to swallow it and throw up? I gag when I brush my teeth, so what's a mouthful of spunk going to be like?

We've got the lights off and just a small lamp in the living room, so the room is lit up by the car headlights as it pulls up onto the drive.

"Fuck, it's my parents. Quick, get your top back on!"

I pull my top on and struggle with the buttons. Why does that get harder, the more of a hurry you're in? One holiday, I had some shorts that buttoned at the side with no zip and nearly pissed myself in a public toilet in Turkey trying to get them down in time.

Alex has just about got his jeans back on and zipped up as we hear the sound of the key in the door. Phew. I wasn't sure I'd made a particularly good impression on Mrs Ryan the first time I met her. I think if our second meeting were to begin with me having a mouthful of her son's dick on her couch, well... I don't think we'd be in 'Oh just call me Sandra' territory for about fifty years.

As they walk in, Alex and I pretend to be engrossed in whatever's on the telly. Turns out the play was terrible and they left early. I realise I do actually feel quite tired and it is only Monday night, so I say goodnight. Alex insists on walking me home. Before going, I hear him in the kitchen with his parents, who have put the kettle on.

"What do you think of her?"

"Seems like a nice girl, son. Have you been studying tonight, then?"

"Yeah. Zoe's dead clever. She's helping me a lot."

I hear Mr Ryan laugh. "Oh yes. I remember when I was your age, all I wanted in a girl was someone who could recite Shakespeare. Still, I'm not sure she's that clever, son. She's got her cardi on inside out."

Oh bollocks. Still, I think it's okay. He's laughing about it in a 'Go on, my son' kind of way. And them coming home early got me out of having to find out if I'm a 'spit or swallow' kind of girl.

After Alex has walked me home, we kiss goodbye and promise to meet for lunch tomorrow. His phone starts ringing. He ignores it and we continue kissing. After a couple of minutes it goes off again, so I give him a final hug goodbye and say he'd better answer it.

He walks away as he takes the call. I decide to watch until he's out of sight, hanging on to every last glimpse of him. It's a quiet evening and there's no traffic in the road so I can hear what he's saying.

"Hiya mate. Yeah, been busy all evening. Tell you what, just been walking my girlfriend home but I'm free to talk now..."

Yeeeeesssss!!!

CHAPTER 4

Life's pretty busy right now. Alex has been my boyfriend – I love saying that! – for nearly a month now, so we've done the obvious things like going bowling (he's rubbish, I beat him easily and I always lose to Jay and Kate), the cinema (we don't like the same films, but we're both united in the belief that sweet popcorn is the only acceptable type, and salted is just wrong) and we've even been out for a meal together!

It was so classy. We went to this place called Le Bistro in town because they had a two-for-one coupon in the paper. It was packed out with people who, like us, obviously couldn't have afforded to be there if it wasn't for the offer, but most of them were a few years older than us. I felt like we were a real, proper couple. I wore a smart dress and he wore a cotton shirt and jacket. I was so proud of him, he looked gorgeous. We both have brown hair and eyes and, in a weird kind of way, I kept hoping someone would ask if we were brother and sister, so I could say, 'Oh no, he's my boyfriend!'

Every night I'm doing something: a couple of nights a week round at his house, pretending to be doing homework, then another couple of nights at home, actually doing the homework (I might be all loved-up but I'm not stupid), nights together at mine if Mum's doing a night shift and tonight... it's my driving lesson.

Why did I start driving lessons in August? If I'd had any sense, I'd have started as soon as I turned seventeen in February when the nights were getting lighter, and hopefully have passed my test ready for a Summer of driving around anywhere I wanted. As it is, I didn't get started 'til the end of a Summer of sitting on boiling hot buses next to some old blokes having their own BO festival, and the nights are getting shorter. The clocks will go back next week and I'll have to do all my lessons in the dark then.

"Come on, turn the wheel, a bit more, give it a bit more gas... and go." I'm driving round the roads of the local park. It's a popular route for driving schools because of the wide, infrequently used roads. Well, infrequent except for various other people from school having their lessons as well.

"That's it. I think you've cracked that one, now, Zoe. Another one to tick off the list. We'll have you ready for your test in no time. Well, before Christmas I reckon."

Tess, my instructor, is brilliant. She's so patient, even when I was turning a corner and went for the accelerator instead of the brake and nearly took out a road island. I'm getting better now, though. I feel loads more confident behind the wheel and I'm managing the manoeuvres with, well, a bit more ease. My sixty-seven point turn is now down to the three it's meant to be, at least.

"So how's things with you, anyway?" she asks. I enjoy our little chats. If you're going to spend two hours a week in a car with someone, especially while you're feeling nervous or stressed about conquering a new skill, it certainly helps if you can get on with them. I had a different instructor before Tess; he was the guy Jay passed with. Jay couldn't recommend him highly enough, but to be honest he gave me the creeps, so I found Tess and haven't looked back since.

"Great," I say with a smile.

To be honest, apart from, "I've got period pain," or, "Oh Sasha, it's you, " I say most things with a smile these days. Just having Alex in my life, knowing he picked me, wanted me as much as I wanted him, makes everything a little bit better.

"I finally got talking to that boy from my English class," I tell her. "We've been going out for about a month. Well, I say going out – it's more staying in, but you know what I mean."

"Oh, I do," she replies. "remember it well. Can he drive yet?"

When I tell her that no, Alex hasn't passed his test yet either, Tess says, "Right, we have to crack on and get you through this test. You don't want him doing it before you, do you? And once you're driving, you can start going out properly. Move on when you're ready..."

Another person who knows about me and Alex now is Mum. We were sitting at home one night, watching her favourite thing, the shopping channel. Don't ask. She's always got it on whenever she's home, and you wouldn't believe some of the stuff she's bought: There's the more obvious stuff like suntan lotion and makeup, but then we've had stuff like fudge making kits, 8000 loom bands (she offered to make me a dress; I offered to put myself up for adoption) and even some rubber purple massage thing (I thought about asking her what it was, but in the end I thought it was better not to know) turn up at the house. Weird.

She justifies it by saying it's not always easy for her to get to the shops when she works shifts, but how does that in any way explain ordering £50 worth of cheese in one go? Anyway, I know it must be serious if she's willing to tear herself away from the orange presenter yakking on about some cream that's taken twenty years off her. I can only assume the woman's actually about 135, then. She reaches for the mute button and tells me she wants to talk about something.

She tells me how she'd spotted a condom wrapper in the bin. Oh hell, I'd always wrapped the condoms in tissue and then disguised them in a carrier bag. Alex must have just put one of the wrappers in the bathroom bin without thinking. Still, I guess this had to come out sometime.

Mum says, "I know you're old enough to have..." she pauses, "to sleep with someone, but as your mother I can't help but feel worried."

"Mum, he's gorgeous," I say. "I fancied him for

ages, and he's really nice to me. You'd like him."

She doesn't look entirely convinced. "So, have you been doing this the whole time I've been working nights? You haven't been in my bed, have you?"

"Oh no, Mum," I tell her. To be honest, I thought she'd be more relaxed about this than she is. "It's only been the last few weeks. We got together at Jay's party. And trust me, there's no way I'll ever think about going into your bed," I say, smiling.

She's not really amused by that, so I decide it might be best to leave out the detail that, never mind the idea of leaving shagging until the third date, me and Alex didn't even have a first date before we did it. Not sure that'll win him any fans, and I'm not sure what she'd say if she knew I pretty much chased after him with one thing in mind.

"Seeing him isn't getting in the way of my school work. I still do all my assignments – in fact, we work together on them."

She raises an eyebrow. "Do you now? Look, Zoe love, I know you're not a little kid, but just be careful. And there's one other thing we should discuss..."

I roll my eyes. "Oh Mum, I'm being careful! I'm not stupid. You found the condom wrapper, didn't you?" This is not a conversation I want to have, believe me. Right now, the prospect of watching old Tango Face on the shopping channel's looking pretty good.

"That wasn't what I was going to say, actually," she replies. "No, we discuss when he's coming round for tea and I'm going to meet this boy."

My mum is the best!

As soon as I can without it looking really obvious, I shoot upstairs and call him. "I've told my mum about us. Yeah, everything... well, more or less. Anyway, she wants you to come round for tea so she can check you out."

I hear him laugh on the other end.

"Great. I was wondering how long I was going to be your dirty little secret."

"Oh, you may have been secret, and definitely dirty, but no way are you little," I tease.

"You dirty mare," he laughs. "Well, is it just an informal thing or will I have to learn about where to put the fish knife? Do I have to rent a tuxedo or can I come in my jeans?"

"You can come any way you like," I giggle, "but

maybe we should wait until after dinner. Seriously, if I were you, I'd try to go for something that says, 'I know I'm doing your baby girl, but honestly, I'm not a psycho' if you can manage it."

"No pressure then, eh? Can't wait. Bye, babe."

CHAPTER 5

Halloween. It's a funny thing. I remember as a little girl, how my parents wouldn't let me go Trick or Treating. I remember how every year, both of them would moan, "It's nothing more than begging! If you want some sweets, I'll buy you some... and then there's taking sweets from strangers! Perhaps we should just go all out and let you play with fire?"

By the time I was about seven, my parents weren't seeing eye- to-eye on most things, but Halloween was one thing they could still agree on. And they agreed to hate it.

I wasn't bothered so much about the sweets, it was the idea of the dressing up I always found attractive. I always wanted to transform myself with a black wig, white face makeup and a stark, red mouth, dripping with blood. I guess it's not too surprising that I tend to fancy Alex most when he's got eyeliner and a hint of eyeshadow on when we go for nights out, and my dress sense has caused me to be labelled 'Emo freak' by Sasha and her henches.

I'm not an emo. I've never dyed my hair and I can't do the makeup to save my life. I just know I look great in black and red, so that's what I tend to wear all the time. So Halloween is a bit like my prom.

Speaking of which, there's a Year 7 Halloween disco on at school and they've asked for people to help out. At this point in Year 13, anything that can be made to sound good on a UCAS form is going to get loads of volunteers. With my talent for English, I'm sure I can turn 'manning the orange squash stall' into something good: 'providing stimulation for the hydrationally-challenged learning cohort', maybe?

It's not about the kids, or even about my UCAS form. I already take part in the school's reading scheme and mentor a couple of kids with special needs to cover that. This is all about the outfit... and not just mine.

Remember how everyone said Alex and I looked sweet and matching when we both turned up in black and red on the night we got together? Well, I want us to recreate that look, wearing the same clothes... but this time, we'll be zombies! The kids will love it at the disco.

When we get back to mine, I'll love it too. Just thinking about it is making me tingle.

I was really nervous about how it'd go when Alex came round to meet my mum. I kept thinking, what if she doesn't like him? There's no way I'd have stopped seeing him, but if she wasn't keen on him, it'd just make things really awkward. I shouldn't have worried though: he charmed the pants off her by talking about how getting his A levels is just as important as his acting, and enthusiastically chewing through a slab of her lasagne, even though it was a bit burnt.

I definitely think she'd warmed to him by the end of the evening, so much so that she's okay with him coming upstairs into my room even while she's at home. Obviously, we don't do anything much, just kissing, but it's great to think she likes him and she's accepted that we're a couple.

Sometimes I can't believe we've only been together for six weeks. I mean, we still rip each other's clothes off the minute we get any time alone, but I feel so comfortable when I'm with him, it's like we've known each other a lot longer. Still, I've learned a lot about him in the last few weeks. I felt I had to make up for a whole year of just gawping at him in English and never finding anything out about him.

Ten things I've learned about Alex Ryan in the last month:

1. His actual name isn't Alexander as I assumed, but Alexei. Turns out his mum's half Russian, and she still loves all things USSR, especially the literature. She named him after one of the main characters in this book she loves called 'Anna Karenina', and partly after herself I suppose, because she's called Alexandra. His brother's even called Leo, after the book's author. I've started reading 'Anna Karenina' myself, and I have to agree, my Alexei is living up to his namesake. Just hope he doesn't also take after his mum too much, I don't want to have to call our first kid bloody Boris Karloff or something.

2. His birthday is December 21st, which he hates for two reasons. One, it's officially the shortest day of the year so he feels cheated, and two, it's so near Christmas it gets swallowed up in last-minute shopping and Christmas parties. Well, all I can say to that is this: try being born on

Valentine's Day, mate! Maybe we should both pick an extra birthday, like the Queen or whatever, and celebrate in some random time like June.

3. He got into acting when he was about eight. His mum kept getting complaints from his primary school about his 'energetic behaviour and being prone to fantasise', so she thought enrolling him in the local drama club might sort him out. Good call from Mrs R, as it turns out.

4. He's been on telly twice: the week-long part as 'Teenage thug' who threw bricks at an old lady's house in the soap I mentioned, and as an extra (supporting artist he calls it) in an advert for headache tablets that required fifty kids all dressed in blue leotards. He's wasn't so forthcoming about that one. His mum showed me a photo of him looking -even I've got to admit- a bit ridiculous.

5. If faced with a bag of Revels, he'd take the orange cream first and not eat the coffee cream... which is great, because I love the coffee and hate the orange. We'd both go for the flat chocolate counter over any of them. I reckon this means we're officially destined to be together, it's written in the stars... or the Galaxy, I suppose.

6. He's not really into football, which I guess is good for him since he spends a lot of Saturdays at his youth theatre group, and sometimes attending auditions.

7. He's got a scar on his left knee from falling out of a tree when he was six.
8. He's got the most amazing eyes that I could just drown in... but I suppose that doesn't count because I knew that before we got together. The only difference is I'm allowed to look at them now without him thinking I'm weird.
9. Same goes for his body.
10. I think I love him.

Love. That's a big word. Well, it is and it isn't. I say it all time: I love that top you're wearing, I love dogs, I love Fridays... but when it will be the right time to say 'I love you, Alex?'

Not yet. No matter how comfortable I feel, the fact remains that we have only been seeing each other for just over a month. I know that's far too soon to come out with the 'L- bomb', don't want to scare him off, do I?

But just because I can't say it, doesn't mean I can't feel it. I'll just keep it to myself.

CHAPTER 6

"This all looks wonderful, girls, you really have done an amazing job. Well done." Mr Burton is walking past the school hall, which has been transformed into a Halloween den of darkness, spiders and cobwebs.

"Boys as well, Sir," Alex calls from the top of a ladder where he's fixing a banner across the stage with Jay.

"Err, yes, boys as well, Alexander," he says. "I'm sure the Year Seven students will have a great time."

Alex rolls his eyes and shakes his head slightly, but presumably decides it's not worth correcting the head.

The hall does look fantastic. The stage is covered in black and orange fabric, there are huge cardboard ghosts tacked onto the velvet curtains and we've got a table set up, where we're going to sell Halloween-themed cupcakes and hotdogs made by the Catering students. It might turn out to be a bad idea, but we've adapted a few Drama games with a Halloween twist to break up the dancing. Just hope the Year Sevens don't think it's too childish. Now all we have to do is get ready.

We have to go to the toilets to change, and it seems a bit silly that Alex and I have to split off and go the boys' and girls' cubicles. I've seen him naked, for God's sake! Still, suppose I don't want everyone else getting a look. He's all mine... and when he comes out, with his suit, white shirt (not the same one as he wore on our first night, this is a cheap one he's covered in fake bloodstains) and a dead rose on his lapel, I feel all the knicker-dampening lust I felt last time. I just want to grab him now. It's going to be hard waiting 'til the disco's over.

He looks at me.

"Whoa. I forgot how good you look in that dress." He comes up close to me and we kiss. And again. Then we risk one more before anyone appears on the corridor. He gives me a smile and a meaningful look. I know what he's thinking.

"No way, Alex. We can't. Imagine Burton walking past and seeing us. He'd fucking die!"

"It'd give the old guy a thrill," he laughs. "I bet he hasn't got his end away since about 1991."

"Well yeah, but..."

I have to admit, it's a tempting thought. I can feel him hardening as we're still standing close together. Could we? No. I know my mum likes Alex, but I don't think even he's got a winning enough smile to calm her down if we got expelled for being caught having the mother of all danger shags.

I give him one more determined kiss and pull away from him.

"Save it for later," I say, gesturing at his hard-on with my eyes. His eyes are fixed on mine with a look of delicious hunger. Like he just wants to eat me. Oh God, he's so sexy I could give in. I want to.

My mind (and the fear of my mum killing me) regains control. I've said no. That's it. But now I just want to get this disco over with so we can be alone.

He gives my bum a playful slap as I turn to head back to the hall. He pulls me back gently by the arm and whispers something as he looks me up and down: "Babe, I am going to fucking destroy you later."

I can't wait.

The next three hours are fun. The kids love our outfits, they're not too old for the games and by the end of the night, there's only about three cupcakes left. This has got to have earned us all at least a paragraph's worth of decent reference comments for our UCAS forms.

Once the last Year Seven has been collected, the caretaker says he'll take down the decorations and clear up, so we're free to go.

At last. We head round to my house, which I know is going to be empty. Obviously, we've both calmed down a bit just by being preoccupied with working on the disco, but we've both still got our earlier conversation in our minds. I can tell because he's walking a lot more quickly than usual.

As soon as I shut the front door and drop my bag, he takes hold of me and presses me up against the wall. His tongue penetrates eagerly in a passionate kiss, whereas the rock-hard erection I can feel against my belly tells me he's ready for action. We throw our coats on the couch and dash upstairs. Neither of us says a word. We don't need to.

We pull our clothes off with a sense of urgency, throwing them to the floor and finally jumping onto the bed with a bounce. I slide my head down towards his groin and start running my hands along his penis.

"Let's do something for you first," I say, looking up at him. He bites his lip and sighs.

I've definitely got better at blowjobs, but I never could face the idea of swallowing. In the end, we've agreed that he can let me know when he's getting there and he finishes himself off by hand, or we do what we're doing now: use it as a warm up before sex.

"Oh God, that's it," he whispers, pushing my head off him carefully. "You're so good at that now. I'm so close I thought I'd better stop you, or I'll have nothing left."

"Yeah, don't you dare," I laugh. "I've been waiting for this all night. I've been surrounded by a bunch of little kids trying to do the 'Thriller' dance, but the whole time, all I could think of was you."

"At least you girls can keep it secret! I've been fighting this boner since we got changed. It's a bloody nightmare! I thought I was going to poke Burton's eye out."

"Urrgh, that's a mental picture I didn't want. Still, you can't put me off. Let's do it."

The we both stop talking as he guides himself inside. Despite his earlier promise, he's actually really gentle, taking time to stroke my body and kiss my neck as he continues thrusting back and forth until we're both finished. We're not just a pair of horny teenagers shagging someone, anyone because we're desperate to do it. As far as I'm concerned, it's only good because it's him. If I couldn't have Alex, I wouldn't want anyone else. It dawns on me that this is it: we're actually making love. It feels so wonderful.

Afterwards, he lies on his back, while I'm on my side, draped over him with my head on his chest. The silence isn't awkward, it's natural. I feel so safe, so happy with him. I love him.

I love him. No getting away from it.

Eventually, we know we've got to move. Neither of us has eaten, so we go downstairs and reheat the pasta Mum left for us on the kitchen counter. We eat in front of the telly.

Putting his fork down on the plate, he says, "That was fantastic."

"I'll tell Mum you liked it. She might do it again for you."

"Not the food, although yeah, say thanks to your mum for me. I mean tonight."

He looks at me.

"You." He pauses a little before saying, "I.."

What? He's not going to say it, is he?

"I love everything we do together."

Oh. The cop-out phrase. Still, tonight has changed things. He may not have said it, but I really feel like we're in love. For real.

CHAPTER 7

I've never liked November. It's the time when it starts getting really cold, really dark and it seemed to last forever when I was a child. A long expanse of time between the fun on Bonfire Night and the excitement of Christmas. I still hate it, even though I'm not writing a Christmas list for Santa anymore. Now, November is all about being skint from having to save up for Christmas presents and the nightmare of Christmas shopping. Any time through the rest of the year, I love a wander round the shops with Jay or Kate, whether we buy anything or not. Mostly it's about relaxing at the weekend and coffee and a chat with my mates. However, from the end of October up until around the first week in January, town on a Saturday becomes a hellish place I'd rather avoid.

This year though, there's a bit more excitement to it: I have to buy a present for my boyfriend! And presumably, he'll get me something. I mean, I don't care about expensive stuff, but I've seen Kate with her gifts for the last couple of Christmases and felt jealous of the fact she had someone willing to give her them. They were usually things I could just get myself, but that's not the point, is it?

After thinking about it for a while, my feeling of excitement turns to vague worry. Will I get him the right thing? I need something that really shows him how I feel, but without being over-the-top or freaking him out... and it's his birthday four days before! I know I've got to avoid the cardinal sin of giving one present to cover both occasions, but that just means double the pressure. How am I going to think of two good presents that really impress him, and that I can afford?

I've got another reason to hate November this year. Alex has got a part in the panto again. Still the chorus, but the lead boy, if you like. He gets a couple of lines and a lot more stage time than the other chorus kids. It's a definite step up, but it's going to mean I won't see as much of him over the next month while he has to rehearse... and then he'll be doing the actual performances once we get to mid-

December. Being with an actor's nowhere near as glamorous as I thought it'd be. I can't wait 'til he's famous and doing films – and he will be, I'm sure of that. I can sit and wait for him on set in a luxury trailer. Oh well, I can dream can't I? I might need to cling onto that thought to get me through a miserable month ahead without seeing him much.

I decide to put it out of my mind and snuggle into Alex's back. He's lying on his side, still asleep. It's a Saturday morning and he slept here again. We come to my house a lot more than his just 'cause Mum's out at work so often. I nuzzle into the back of his neck. I love the way he smells, even first thing in the morning.

When he wakes up, he gets a shower while I make us both some breakfast. You know, much as I love Mum and everything, I find myself imagining what it'd be like if she wasn't here. That this was our place, just me and Alex. Living together. I think we could do it.

After breakfast, we head off on the bus into town. He's going to the theatre to get started, I'm meeting Jay and Kate. Hopefully they can give me some ideas for the two presents I need to start looking for, and maybe on another, slightly more important matter...

We usually meet up at this little place called Café Italia. We never go to any of the big high street chains. I could try to sound all principled and make out I'm all about supporting the small local business, but really it's because their caramel lattes are seventy pence cheaper than the chains, and just as yummy.

While I'm waiting for them, I spend a few minutes messing around on my phone. Since it seems to be the only thing on my mind at the moment, I ask Google: How do you know if someone loves you?

After about ten minutes, all I can conclude is that a) It's impossible to say, as there's no one way in which we all feel or show love, and b) This doesn't stop a lot of people on the internet talking bollocks about it. Anyway, I'm none the wiser.

Jay arrives first, with Connor, whom he kisses goodbye before he leaves to start his afternoon shift at Macdonalds. It seems my flirting with Alex at the party back in September did spark off a bit of a discussion between Jay and his parents. It turns out they had an idea Jay was gay for about the last year, and all the comments about me were to see if they could prompt him into saying anything. I'm just glad they're fine with it and Jay can be himself now.

"What's up, Zo?" he asks me. "For someone who's got a hot new fella, you're looking a bit miserable."

God, is it that obvious? I stir the sprinkles into my coffee, but don't reply. I'm not really sure what to say. If I can't talk to Jay about it though, who can I talk to?

"Jay, I know it's only been a couple of months, but I think I love him."

"Ah, now I understand. You don't want to be the first to say it."

"I can handle being first to say it, just what if I'm the only one who says it? What if he doesn't love me? About two weeks ago, the night of the kids' disco, I thought he was going to say it, but,"

Jay winces. "He didn't say, 'I love spending time with you', did he?" The look on his face shows he's feeling a bit sorry for me right now.

"He might as well have done. It was, 'I love everything we do together'. What does that even mean? It means he likes watching films and shagging. It doesn't mean he loves me."

Kate's here now, and after I fill her on mine and Jay's conversation so far, she says, "Look,

Zo. I wouldn't worry about it too much. He's with you, isn't he? And I know it seems like ages, but it still is a fairly short time to say you love someone."

"Doesn't feel like it to me. I..." I hover a little bit, surprising myself, "I know I love him."

Kate smiles at me like I'm a small child. I hate it when she does that. Just 'cause she's been with Danny for nearly two years, sometimes she thinks she knows it all. She looks at Jay.

"Hmmm. What do you think, Jay? I think we need to apply the acid test: answer these questions, no hesitation. Question one... has he seen you eat a wrap?"

"Ha! Yes he has! And he still wanted to kiss me afterwards!"

I'll admit I can get a bit messy when I eat wraps, especially when we went to this street food van that does really big ones. I've only got little hands and stuff was falling out everywhere. He even went and got his phone out and took a picture of me with sauce on my face, the bastard.

"Alright, what about this? Have you been round to see his family? I don't just mean a brief introduction, I mean, has he shown you off to his nan and everyone?"

Again, I don't have to hesitate.

"Yes, actually," I can reply with a smug tone, feeling this conversation is going the way I want it to. "I went to his cousin's 21st about three weeks ago, remember? You helped me pick out that red underwear set."

"Oh yeah, so I did."

Am I imagining it, or does she sound disappointed? Does she want to prove he doesn't love me or something?

"Okay, not bad... but what about the third and final question? This is the big one. Does he still come around when you're on,"

"Urrgh, girls, do you mind?" Jay interrupts.

"Does he still come around when you're on, and he knows nothing's going to happen?"

That's been the biggest thing so far, I admit. I mean, I've only had three periods since we've been together. The first time was when I'd only been with him for two weeks, so I lied and just said I was too busy for him to come around. Then next time, we'd been together six weeks by that point and I thought, unless he totally failed Biology, he must know this is going to happen – in fact, it'd be more of a problem if it didn't! I decided to warn him when it was blob time, imagining he'd stay away. He didn't, though.

I smile.

"Yeah, he does... although that's not to say nothing happens," I say, poking my tongue into the side of my mouth. I suddenly realise what I've done, and how it does make it sound a bit like Alex is still only coming round because there'd be something on offer sex-wise, so I add, "but we sometimes just watch a film if I'm feeling rotten."

I have done a few things for him when I'm on the blob, but only if I want to. He never pressures me.

"Impressive," Kate concludes. "Well, I know I'm no expert, but I think if he doesn't actually love you yet, he's getting there."

As we get up to leave, she says, "I'm so glad he passed the test. I can see you've really fallen for him, so he'd better be good enough."

At five o'clock I've got another driving lesson. I'd guess Tess is about late thirties, but I like meeting up with her and talking while I practise. It's like she's become another friend. She always asks how my A levels are going, I regale her with tales of whatever weird shit Mum's bought off the shopping channel this week, and of course I've told her about Alex. In fact, she was one of the first to know about him, back at the end of the Summer holidays when I was wondering whether to make Year 13 the year I went for it and approached him. I didn't want to tell Mum, I was nervous about admitting it to my mates: the driving instructor seemed like a nice, safe person to let it all out to.

"Well, if your friends think he might love you, that's a good sign," she says agreeably.

I didn't tell her exactly what Kate's criteria were, just that he passed them all.

"Can I suggest something? If I were you, I'd hold on until Christmas, and didn't you say it's his birthday around that time as well? When you sign his cards, put 'Love from' on it. Then you can see what he writes on yours. If he writes, 'Love' as well, it could be time to talk about it, and if he doesn't, then you can just pass the fact you wrote 'Love' off as something lots of people do on cards."

The woman's a genius.

"That's really not a bad idea, Tess. Thanks."

"I'm full of them... and do you know what

else? I think you're ready for your test."

Really? No way! I do feel confident driving around and doing my manoeuvres now, but am I ready to go for it? After a few minutes reflection, I decide it wouldn't be the scariest thing I've done this year.

"I've been in touch with the test centre, and they've got a cancellation on the 3rd of December. Do you want me to book it for you?"

Oh my God! I could get my driving licence before Christmas! Just in time to drive myself off a cliff if Tess's suggestion goes tits up...

CHAPTER 8

After collecting the opinions of Kate, Jay and Tess, you'll notice there's one person I still haven't spoken to about the whole Love thing: my mum.

After our initial chat, we've had some kind of silent agreement that we won't talk about me having sex at all. She seems satisfied to know we use condoms, and that Alex is a sensible boy who respects me. Anything else, she doesn't need to know.

But what about whether he loves me or not? Surely she'd want to think he does... but then, I know my mum. If you were to ask her, 'Does my bum look big in this?', if it does, she'll let you know. She's not nasty or rude, but she's definitely honest. And I'm not sure I want to face it if she says she doesn't think he loves me, because I know she'd be right.

Although I may not want to face it, my curiosity is driving me mad, so I decide to go for another approach. It's a Tuesday night, Alex is rehearsing and I'm watching 'Holby City' (Why would any nurse want to watch that? It must feel like homework, but she loves it) with Mum.

"Mum? Can I ask you something?"

"Of course, love." She pauses the telly.

"How did you know you loved Dad?"

She lets out a long breath. I very rarely mention my father to her. We haven't seen him for years; he's missing, presumed useless. He just said he was going out one day when I was eight and never returned. Things hadn't been good between them for some time, but you can imagine how hard it would have been for Mum, wondering where on earth he was.

About four months later he wrote and told her he was alive and that she shouldn't be worried about him. Trust me, she certainly wasn't by that time. Since then, Mum's had the odd boyfriend, but I suppose she doesn't want to let anyone else hurt her the way Dad did.

She must have loved Dad once, though. At the

start, when they were first going out. When I was born. There must have been some good times.

She gets up from the armchair, then comes and sits next to me on the couch.

"Zo, I know this is going to be hard for you to hear, but looking back, I don't think I ever did. He certainly didn't love me if he could sod off and leave like he did."

I've no idea what my face looks like, but she can see I'm shocked. She puts her arm round me and says, "I'm sorry love, but I suppose you should know the truth. I want you to be absolutely sure you love someone before you get married, or have kids, or anything, Zo. I mean, I've got you and that's the only real positive I can say there was, but there's so many things we've both missed out on."

When she says 'we', does she mean me and her, or her and Dad? I can't think straight right now.

"What about at the start?" I ask, desperate for some reassurance. "It must have been good then. Why did you have me if it was as bad as that?"

"I'm not saying it was always bad, love. He was never violent and he wasn't a drinker, nothing like that. I just... never got the feeling we were what he really wanted. Fair enough, he could have just buggered off when I told him I was pregnant with you, but I sometimes think maybe he should have done. Especially if he was only going to do it eight years later. And I do blame myself. I often wonder, could I have tried harder, but how can you really love someone if you know, deep down, that they don't love you?"

She looks at me. "Why are you asking me this?"

I'm a bit too stunned from her bombshell to answer. It seems she works it out anyway.

"You're in love with your Alex, aren't you? Well, from everything I've seen of him, he's a good lad. Just take your time and don't make the mistakes I made."

I tell Mum I'm going upstairs to watch something else in my room, but I'm sure she knows that isn't true. As soon as I shut my bedroom door, the tears come. I always knew Mum and Dad didn't get on - they wouldn't be the first, loads of people I know have parents who've broken up, it's often the best thing - but to have never loved him in the first place?

What does that make me? A nuisance that stopped Mum leaving him and having her own life, or to put it the other way, the thing that kept Dad locked in a miserable marriage for so long? I just feel like the few good memories I do have – did have - have just become worthless. None of it was true if they didn't love each other even then.

Am I being a total idiot hoping Alex loves me? Maybe it's all pointless and no-one really loves anyone. Maybe I should forget about love. I did fine without it for seventeen years.

No, that's not true, I tell myself, picking up my phone. I leave him a voicemail:

"Alex? It's me. Call me when you're finished, don't care how late. I'll still be up. Bye."

I drop my phone on the bed and continue sobbing quietly. I know Mum was only being honest (it's what she does best, as well as buying shite off the telly) but I really don't want to be with her right now.

After about twenty minutes, I hear the doorbell.

It's him. I stand at the top of the stairs and listen. I still don't want to go down and see Mum just yet.

"Hi, Gemma." Mum's insisted he call her by her first name since that first night he came round for tea, armed with a £5 bunch of flowers from Aldi. "Look, I know it's late, but can I see Zoe? She just called me, and well, she sounded pretty down. So down I didn't want to wait 'til tomorrow."

"Sure, go ahead," Mum says, not exactly in the usual cheery tone she saves for visitors. "She's upstairs."

He comes up. He's wearing a white T-shirt, grey jogging pants and a zip-up hoodie with the logo of his drama academy on it. Maybe they've been practising the dance sections tonight.

"Alex? You didn't have to come," I say with a wobbly voice.

"Yes I did," he says. "What's wrong?"

I open my mouth to tell him and I can't speak. I just start crying again. He steps forward and puts his arms around me, kissing the top of my head.

"Hey, hey, come on. Tell me about it." More gentle kisses. "There's got to be something I can do."

I tell him about what Mum said. He's sympathetic, but I can see he's trying to find a solution. Something positive to say.

"Your mum never said they didn't love you, just that they didn't love each other."

We're sitting on my bed now, and I've calmed down a bit.

"I know this has been hard, Zo, but would you have preferred her to lie? Let you think everything was great when it really wasn't?"

"I'm not sure," I say. "Of course I've known she hasn't cared about him for years, but how could they be together when they didn't love each other? Why did they have me?"

He's silent for a minute. "Well, I can't answer either of those questions, but I know I'm glad they had you," he says, planting a kiss on my forehead. "I couldn't imagine life..."

He pauses again. Why does he struggle to tell me how he feels? Am I that unlovable?

He takes my face in his hands, looking me straight in the eyes. He wipes away the tear that wells up in one of my eyes and says,

"Oh Zo, I just want to make love to you right now. I don't care if your mum hears us."

He's said this to me once before: on our first night. That time it would have just been so I didn't tell everyone that the famous Alex Ryan, the future film star, was less 'Lethal Weapon' and more 'Gone in Sixty Seconds'... and maybe, now I know him, to make me feel a bit better about dropping my pants the night I got off with him, but this time it feels real. He's not bullshitting me to get into my knickers: he means it.

I mean, I'm hardly at my most attractive tonight. My eyes are all red and I'm wearing the thick fleece pyjamas I wear to lounge around the house in on Winter nights. I think could only look less sexy if I had a massive bogey hanging out of my nose... which starts running almost on cue from the crying, so I have to reach across him and grab a tissue from my dressing table.

Either he really does care about me, or it's true what they say about how teenage boys will shag anything with a pulse.

"I just want to make you feel better," he whispers, stroking the side of my face and leaning in to give me another kiss. "Come on. It's going to be alright."

Even though Mum's downstairs, we pull back the covers and everything he does is about me.

Afterwards, we hold each other and I think about what just happened. He's here, when he doesn't need to be; I didn't ask him to come. I was in a mess, at my absolute worst and he still wanted to be with me. If that's not love, then what is?

Maybe he's never said those three little words, but perhaps I need to stop being so neurotic about it.

He's up early the next morning. I want to walk to school with him, but he needs to go home and change before lessons, because he's still in his rehearsal gear from last night. I kiss him goodbye at the top of the stairs and then continue getting dressed. He passes my mum, who's putting her makeup on in the hall mirror.

"Are you off, then? How's she feeling?"

"A bit better, I think. You should ask her, really." He might get on okay with Mum, but I can see why he'd feel uncomfortable discussing this.

"Yeah well, I've never wanted to give you the whole heavy-handed 'You-hurt-my-princess-and-I'll hunt-you-down' talk, but I will say this: I had my life ruined by a man. If anyone ever does that to her..."

I can hear the surprise in his voice. "What?

You've got nothing to worry about from me, Gem, er, Ms Thompson." I guess he feels the first-name privileges have been suspended for this conversation. "There's no way I'd ever hurt Zoe. I really, really care about her."

"Fine. Just promise me one thing. Don't ever say you love her unless you mean it. Just don't mess her around. I think one man who did that to her is enough, don't you?"

He agrees and then leaves. Well, after last night I feel a lot more secure about us, but having had that little warning, I wonder how long I may have to wait to hear the boy I love say he loves me too?

But then, as I finish getting dressed, I remind myself of last night. Maybe he's not saying it: he's just doing it.

CHAPTER 9

In my life, I've faced some nervous situations.
There was that time a couple of years ago
when I was home alone and thought someone
was in the back garden. I spent ages hovering
by the curtains, not sure I could risk opening
them for a look. When I did, it turned out the
noise had been caused by the plastic patio
furniture falling over. Still, shit me up big time
all the same.

I was nervous the night I pursued Alex.
Looking back, now we've been together for
three whole months and we're in 'neither one
of us is saying it, but I feel like it's love', I find
it hard to think I was ever nervous around
him, but I was.

These things, however, have got absolutely
nothing on the nerves I'm feeling now, as I sit

in the driving test centre.

My head's telling me there's no reason to be nervous, I'm calm and controlled on the roads and can reverse park with my eyes shut – okay, bad comparison, but you know what I mean. I'm fine is what I'm saying. That's with Tess, though. Today I'll have to please some weird examiner I've never met before.

Why can't you do the test with your instructor? Why do you have to do it with some stranger? The only time I can imagine I might ever need to drive with someone I don't know in the passenger seat will be if I ever get hijacked, and I think you could forgive me the odd messy gear-change in that situation...

"Miss Thompson?"

I look up from the floor, which I've been carefully examining since I arrived. This is the person who's going to decide my fate today; whether tonight's spent getting estimates for car insurance, or sitting in my room with Kate slagging them off for being a miserable bastard and failing me.

Hmm. It's a man and let's just say, he doesn't exactly look like he's going to be my new best friend. In fact, he doesn't look like he does friendly at all.

"Right, Miss Thompson, or can I call you Zoe? My name's Malcolm Webber and I'm going to be your examiner today. Do you have your provisional licence, please?

"Err, yeah, sure." This was about the documents, but he takes it as permission to call me Zoe as well. Fine. Whatever. I don't really care. Suddenly, I'm shaking almost visibly and I'm afraid I might be sick.

"Can you lead me out to your vehicle, please?"

You know what, I'm not bloody sure, but I'll give it a go. I shuffle out to Tess's driving school car and then he asks me to read a number plate of some other car on the other side of the car park.

Phew. At least I got that right. There's a girl at school for who, when she got to this bit of the test, found out she's blind as a bat and has needed glasses for ages. She couldn't make out any of the numbers. Bloody hell, it's amazing she got as far as applying for the test without crashing. Anyway, not only did she have to get the glasses, but she failed the test and lost the fee. That's another thing. I think you should only have to pay the fee if you pass the test. Having to pay out £62 to be allowed to do something your instructor can verify that you can already do – drive - is bad enough, but to pay all that money and not even be allowed to drive at the end of it...

I can't let that happen. I take a deep breath. I'm going to pass the hell out of this test. I put the key in the ignition, look around everywhere except up Malcolm bloody Webber's left nostril and begin moving the car through the gates of the test centre.

It's a surprisingly sunny day for December, and the sun's reflecting off the windscreen. Once again, I curse myself for not starting the lessons earlier, so I could have taken my test some other time. As we drive along, I try to look at what this guy's writing on the sheet he's got fixed to a clipboard. Damn. I can't, I'd have to take my eyes off the road to see it. When we stop at some lights, l risk a peep that might even last a whole second but I still can't make anything out. The sly bastards probably use some sort of code to stop anyone working out how it's going before the end of the test anyway.

I might be determined, but that doesn't make me any the less nervous. Still, I'm doing my best to concentrate and get everything right. Tess told me I can chat to the examiner if I want, but they won't say anything to me (apart from test instructions) unless I start a conversation. Hmm, not sure making small talk with Malcolm's going to do much to help me, so I just stare straight ahead.

Fuck. Fucking bollocks. We've turned round a corner, and I did indicate, but I've just realised we're halfway down the road and the left indicator's still on. He's going to fail me for this, isn't he? I turn the indicator off and he says, "Why did you do that, Zoe?"

I want to say, 'Why do you think, dickhead? Because we're halfway down the road and I turned ages ago', but instead I mumble, "Because I've finished the left turn, and to avoid other drivers thinking I was going to pull over."

"Right. Take the right turn ahead and park in one of the bays."

We're heading back to the test centre. I nearly made it, but I've messed it up in the last five minutes. All that time spent practising. Tess'll be disappointed. Then there's the money! Today alone, with two hours' hire of the car and then the test fee, has cost a bomb. I might as well have thrown it all in the bin. Oh well, at least the bottle of wine Mum got me this morning (she said it was for me and Kate to celebrate, but it'll be for drowning my sorrows now) was only a fiver.

My eyes well up. I wish I was one of those

people who can stay in control all the time and never give away what they're thinking, but I just can't. I park the car and then collapse into a blubbering heap. Tess comes out of the centre, and I can see she's obviously concerned.

"That's the end of the test, Zoe. I'm pleased to tell you that you have passed."

I turn and look at Malcolm, open-mouthed. "But what about that indicator?"

"It was an error, but you rectified your mistake and were able to explain why you needed to so," he says, starting to fill in a form. "Now, here's your certificate..."

I'm in total shock. I've only gone and passed first time.

I imagined (when I let myself imagine it) that I'd be driving home, grinning ear to ear, having ripped the L plates off Tess's car. It doesn't happen that way in reality. I'm happy, but I'm still blubbing like a baby and, pass or fail, it seems the instructor always drives someone home after their test. Tess said it's in case they have an accident because they're on such a high, they mightn't be giving the road their full attention. Whatever, I've passed!

When we pull up outside my house, she congratulates me and says, "This is where we normally arrange the next lesson, but well, this time, it's where we say goodbye. I've really enjoyed helping you pass, Zoe. Safe driving."

She gives me some flyers with a discount for motorway lessons and one bigger ordinary flyer, asking me to put it on the noticeboard at school, and then she's gone.

I feel really sad all of a sudden. Of course I've been dying to pass my test, but of course it means no more Tess. I'll miss her.

I come into the house, where Mum's having a cup of tea with Kate. They can see I've been crying, so neither of them speak when I come in. It obviously doesn't look great, but then they know I can cry at anything, so they're probably not sure what to think.

Don't worry, I'm not going to do the 'pretend I've failed and then surprise them' thing. That's so stupid.

"I did it," I say, allowing myself to laugh.

"Oh Zo, that's fantastic! Nice one, babe!" Kate hugs me.

"Now you'll really start learning to drive, when you're out on your own," Mum says.

Why does my Mum always have to find the negative side to everything? Still, I don't care right now.

I tell them about the test, including the bit where I thought I'd screwed it up, then I realise I haven't told Alex yet. It's four o'clock now, so I send him a text in case he's gone to the theatre after school.

The wine gets opened, and Kate, Mum and I have a glass each (why do they always say you get six glasses to a bottle on the label? You don't, our glass each pretty much uses it up) before it's time for Kate to go home.

Mum decides we should get a takeaway and another bottle of wine as it's a special occasion. She's pretty smart when it comes to alcohol. I guess that comes from having to spend her weekends dealing with teenagers who drink bottles of cheap, strong booze in the park and then end up poisoning themselves. Since I was about fifteen, she's been happy for me to have the odd drink at home as long as I don't go mad, and it stays at home.

She offers to walk round the block to get them, since it's my celebration and anyway, I wouldn't get served by our local shopkeeper who knows how old I am. She's only been gone about ten minutes, when there's a knock at the door. Alex.

"Hi, Zo." He grins and gives me a tight hug, before giving me a rather sloppy kiss. "I'm made up for you."

We sit down and I go through the details of my test for him, from the panic in the waiting room, up to the sadness I felt at saying goodbye to Tess.

"So glad you did it. I can give you this now," he says, pulling out a card and a small box from his rucksack.

The card's a typically daft cartoon drawing of a girl driving a car, with an L plate with a big rip drawn down the middle of it. Inside he's written, 'I knew how much this meant to you, so I always knew you'd do it. Alex.'

Alex. Just Alex. I'm not even sure if the squiggle at the end is a wonky, non-committal greeting card kiss, or he's written 'Alexei'.

Don't be stupid, Zoe, I tell myself. He's an actions, not words kinda guy. Remember the night you got upset with Mum? Wasn't that enough proof for you?

"Open the box now," he says, placing it in my hand. I open it, aware that his eyes are watching mine for the reaction.

It's a small, round, silver object attached to a hoop, also made of silver. A keyring. For my first set of car keys when I get them, presumably. That's a really sweet idea. I love it. And I love the fact that if he only found out I passed about an hour ago, he'd obviously bought this already. There'd be no way he could have been into town and back. He believed I'd do it.

"It's lovely, Alex, thanks," I say, then I spot the engraving. On one side it's got *'3rd December'* and on the other it says *'XY,Z'*.

Okay, today's date is straightforward enough (and even more proof of his faith in me, he'd have had to have got that done in advance), but what about the other side? What's the significance of the last three letters of the alphabet, and what's with the comma?

He takes a deep breath before answering me.

"It's not a letter X, it's a kiss, which is a symbol for, for love," he says, "so XY,Z stands for Love You, Zo."

I can't believe what I've just heard. My heart's on fire and I know it sounds ridiculous, but I really do feel like I've got butterflies in my stomach.

He's finally said it.

But how can I know this isn't just a greetings card 'I love you', like Tess said? I'm silent for a few seconds, while I try to think of what I can say.

I finally come out with, "What, love as in..."

"As in, I've never said this to anyone before. It's what it says. I love you, Zoe."

He's the nervous one now, fiddling with the zip on his jacket. "You may not feel the same, because I know it hasn't been that long, but I just wanted to you to know." His eyes dart away from mine to the floor.

"Of course I love you, Alex," I whisper, putting down the keyring and taking him in my arms. With the side of my face against his chest, I can feel his heart racing as well. He's serious.

He loves me. And I've passed my driving test first time. This might just be the best day of my life.

CHAPTER 10

It's been a whole month since I started to think about the two presents I need to get for Alex, and as I'm wandering round Debenhams, I still haven't had any inspiration. I need some quickly, there's only a week to go until the day I'll give him the first one: his birthday.

Of course there are loads of things I'd like to give him – a holiday away somewhere hot, just the two of us, where we could be together all day every day, no school or parents; the keys to a top-spec Nissan Skyline, his dream car... or even just hand him an envelope, but then in the envelope there'd be a card telling him I could pay for him to go to RADA – paying for it'd be the only problem, him getting in is no obstacle in my mind.

However, when you're a skint seventeen-year-old, your options are a lot more limited. I want to get him something that only his girlfriend could give him, but that does NOT mean the cheap, tacky boxer shorts sets with such gems of wit as 'Danger: May Contain Nuts' written on them in the gift department, and I don't think a personalised beer glass is really his thing either.

It's going to be aftershave, isn't it? A boring idea, but at least I know he'll use it. Still, I think I'll have to make that his Christmas present and get something else for his birthday. We're going to have loads of Christmases together, but he's only going to be eighteen once.

Did I just say that? Wow.

I've seen the one he uses on his dressing table, on one of the rare times I've been able to stay at his house, so I leave Debenhams and go to the discount perfume shop and buy the largest bottle I can afford.

Next to the perfume place there's a jeweller's. Not a really pricey, posh one, more like one of those ones where 50% of the stock retails for less than a tenner. I've had the odd pair of earrings from there. Desperate, I look in the window. There's the usual charm bracelets, christening bangles and Diamondesque (who are they kidding?) earrings, but then, on a pad towards the back of the window, there's a few pieces labelled 'For the man in your life.'

There's a silver chain. Or at least, it's silver in colour, but on reading a tiny sticker on the pad I see it's actually white gold. It's not too thick or too delicate, and hanging from it is what I think is a letter from the Russian alphabet. And most important, while it's one of the shop's more expensive items, it's a price I can afford. Just about. My Alexei's going to love it.

Now all I have to do is think of some way to make his birthday the best day of his life. That's going to be even harder than finding the right gift. Being only four days before Christmas, he's going to be spending the day itself doing two performances of the panto. It was the first night yesterday and it's running until January 4th. Even his parents have agreed to put off celebrating his birthday with a family restaurant meal until mid-January.

Still, there's one thing I can do for him that his parents can't... not that I've been doing much of it lately. He's been so busy with the show. I've accepted that (well, what choice do I have?) but my heart misses him. My body misses him... and right now, I'm missing his body big time.

I reach into the bag that contains his bottle of aftershave. The girl who served me popped a couple of samples of toiletries of the same fragrance into the bag. I was going to keep them at my house for him to use when he stays over, but instead I pull the top off the tiny bottle of pure aftershave (I could only afford the EDP, and that was splashing out for me) and inhale, hoping the smell of him will satisfy me. It doesn't. When you're hungry, does thinking about food make you feel any better?

It's no good. I pick up my phone and call him.

"Hello?" We've spoken every night, even if only for a couple of minutes, but I've still missed that voice.

"It's me, Alex. What are you doing?"

"Not much. Slept in, I needed to. I was knackered after the show. Just having a coffee and waking up."

"Is there anyone there with you or," I take a breath, hopefully, "are they all out Christmas shopping?"

I hear him breathe in sharply on the other end of the phone. He knows where this is going.

He pauses for a second, before saying, "Well, Mum and Dad have gone to the Trafford Centre. Leo's Scout troop are doing carol singing there, so they thought they'd take him and do some shopping while they were at it. So I'm all on my own for the next few hours 'til I head off for today's show. Why do you ask?"

Like he doesn't know.

"I'm coming over. That okay?"

"Sure. Any particular reason?" he asks, coyly.

Ooh, the git. He's playing with me.

I look around. I'm sat on a bench in the middle of a pedestrianised high street on the second to last Saturday before Christmas, so I doubt anyone's watching me, but I still don't want anyone else hearing my reply. I lean in to my phone, put my hand over my mouth and, just about louder than a whisper, say:

"I am going to come over there and I'm going to fuck your brains out."

"Oh babe, you say the sweetest things. See you soon," he says, with his sexy laugh.

I hang up, put my phone back in my pocket and flag down a taxi.

Time to open a few presents early.

I arrive at his house after a ten minute ride. During that time, I make sure his presents are hidden in my bag (good job I went for two small items) and he sends me a text telling me that the front door will be unlocked and that I should just come straight up. The text's signed with 'XY,Z', as was my reply, but from me the comma is like when you sign your name on a card, so it's 'Love you (from) Zo'. It's become our thing.

I know he said to come straight in, but it still feels strange opening someone else's front door and just walking in. What if the parents have come home early? Let's face it, we know they've got form for that sort of thing. No, he'd have sent another text.

His house keys are on the coffee table, and his text gave instructions to lock the door after me. I do so, leave my coat and bag downstairs and go up to his room. When I get to his bedroom door, I knock and ask if it's okay to come in. Hey, I might have just offered to fuck his brains out, but there's no need for a girl to forget her manners.

He's lying on his bed. Totally naked.

I think it's safe to say he's pleased to see me. And, just in case you're in any doubt, by that I mean his dick is hard and standing almost upright, not that he's smiling. Although he is also smiling. He does this gorgeous lopsided smile when he's excited. I know he's gagging for it.

"Hiya, babe. I believe you said there was something you wanted to do to me?"

I pull my clothes off as fast as I can and lie next to him. It's only been about ten days since I've been alone with him, but it's felt like a lot more. We begin with a close embrace. I feel his penis up against my naked skin. I don't want to wait much longer.

"God, I've missed you," he says. "I've been wanking myself to a foam over the last week."

"Tell me about it."

I said that because I know how he feels, but actually I don't masturbate. I think I must have been put off by that time with the toothbrush case, because it really doesn't do anything for me. As far as I'm concerned, the thing that makes sex great is being with him – if I'm on my own, it's just messing with myself. What's the point of that? I'm not bothered. Just as we're always being told it's healthy and normal to masturbate, I reckon it's just as healthy and normal if you don't really want to.

Doesn't mean I haven't been driving myself mad thinking about him all week though. I can't wait any more. I lie on my back, ready for him to get on top.

"Erm, Zo. Would you be interested in doing something a bit different?"

"Anything except that bloody reverse cowgirl," I laugh. We looked up some different positions once, and honestly, who wants to be seen from that angle?

"No, not that," he says, picking up a can of spray cream from the floor on his side of the bed.

Well, this is something we haven't done before... and I don't need long to think about it. I adapt something we've both heard Miss Dey say when she's having a bad day. I'm breaking into an embarrassed laugh as I tell him, "Cream me up, Scotty."

What follows is the most intensely erotic experience of my life. He deftly creates circles of cream around each of my nipples, before licking them off with a quick circling motion which makes me giggle at first, but then leaves me shivering with delirium. He then draws a wavy line down the front of my body, which again, he removes with his lovely, eager tongue. Lastly, he makes his way to the foot of the bed, pulls my feet down so my legs are hanging over the edge, and shakes the can, ready to apply some more.

"Oh, fuck me," I sigh, not sure I can handle another orgasm. I was so ready to go by the time I got to his house, it didn't take long.

He looks up at me from where he's kneeling between my legs.

"Oh I will, babe, don't you worry about that. Just one more thing I have to do first."

He laughs. "When I was a kid I used to love those long doughnuts with the cream in the middle," and he begins licking intently, teasing every one of my nerve endings 'til my back arches and I scream with a weird mixture of pleasure and emotion. I'm absolutely destroyed.

He wipes his mouth and climbs on top of me, his face an inch above mine. His voice is low, deliberate and just so horny I want him to fuck me right now. I'm open-mouthed, nearly panting with lust.

"Well, I've eaten, but what about you? Are you hungry? You sounded hungry on the phone."

For a second I think this means it's my turn to spray him with the cream, but he guides himself inside me and gives me a fast, hard shag that makes me climax in less than a minute.

When he climbs off me, I'm speechless. He cuddles into me, with his head on my boobs and says with a smile in his eyes, "Well, was that alright for you?"

"You know damn well it was. Bloody hell, Alex."

"Only the best for you, Zo." For the first time since I arrived, he twists his head up and gives me a warm, loving kiss.

We spend about half an hour in bed. I ask him about how the show went, then we nip downstairs – him in his jogging pants, me in his dressing gown – and get a sandwich because it occurs to us that we are actually hungry. Then, he looks at the time.

"I'm going to have to start getting ready now, babe. There's a matinee show on today."

He walks towards me. "I'm going to hop in the shower, but…"

He pushes his dressing gown off my shoulder and starts kissing my neck, which is a bit sticky from our creamy games earlier. He adopts that low, determined voice again.

"You're all dirty as well. You are one very dirty girl. Someone should give you a good wash... with loads of bubbles." He gives me a hard stare, and the side of his mouth rises into that sexy smile. Then, with a tone of mock despair in his voice, he pulls me close up to his body and says, "What *am* I going to do with you?"

We kiss again, this time lasting for several seconds. I feel my boobs tingling and he's getting a hard-on again.

No way! We're not going to do it in the shower, are we? I've wanted to try it when he's over at mine, but the cubicle's not really big enough. He's got one of those double-size ones that we could both fit in.

We run upstairs and he gets the water just right: hot, but not too hot. Then he puts a condom on. Sure enough, it'd be pretty impossible to do it when we're in there. Lastly, he steps in and leaves the door open for me.

Let's do this.

The water feels wonderful as it drenches us, rinsing off the traces of stickiness. There's a bottle of purple shower gel, which I guess must belong to his mother. I squirt a blob onto my hand, then start massaging his chest and back, making sure I give his nipples lots of attention. I then move my hand down and lather his balls gently. I can tell he's loving it.

He has to bend his legs a little to get inside me, and it's a bit tricky, but it's worth it. We lean against the wall and he thrusts deep into me, each time making me moan softly 'til I can't take any more. He follows me a few seconds after.

When we've both got dressed, it's time to say goodbye. We hug each other, promise to speak before we go to sleep and I wish him the best for his show. It's like the two people shagging furiously in his room and the shower only minutes before, and the boy and girl swapping "I love you"s at the bus stop are two entirely different couples. I can't believe how lucky I am: I'm getting incredible sex from this insanely hot boy, and we love each other as well.

That's what so amazing about us. I love him, he loves me; we can spend hours just holding each other, not saying anything... but this afternoon's shown me that just because you're in love, that doesn't mean the sex can't still be mind-blowing.

The only thing that could make it better is if it was Christmas next week.

CHAPTER 11

December 21st begins with a cold, wet start. I can hear the rain battering against my bedroom window.

I'm lying in my bed, alone, wondering if Alex is awake yet. He probably isn't; last night's show might have ended at half past nine, but by the time he'd have changed, got home and let the adrenaline drain out of his system, he probably didn't get to bed until quite late.

At least I can stay in bed and don't have to get up yet. The school term finished yesterday, so I'm off now until January 5th. I know Alex hates his birthday being where it is, but he did admit he's only ever had to be in school on his birthday once. Still, it does mean he has to spend it working, at least while he's on the way up and having to take lowly chorus parts. He won't be doing that forever though; I know it.

My plans to do something to make his
birthday a day to remember have come to
nothing: largely because it's nearly Christmas
and you can't book a restaurant table
anywhere, and if you could all you'd be able to
get would be a sub-standard office-party
Christmas dinner; partly because he's working
in the afternoon and evening and also because
he's spending the bit of time he does have off
with his family. Well, I suppose they knew him
first. I'm just going to have to make sure we
do something extra-special together in the new
year.

The only thing I'm going to be able to do is pop
by and give him his present at around eleven
o'clock. Possibly his grandparents, and
certainly his parents are going to be there, so
I'll definitely be playing the sweet, respectable
girlfriend who's 'courting' their son, and just
talk a lot about my A levels and baking cakes,
or whatever they want to hear.

Then, for the evening, I haven't told him this
but I'm going to see him in the panto. Last
year, I had to pretend to be taking my cousin,
but this time I've roped Kate and Jay in. We're
going to shout 'Boo!' and 'He's behind you!' as
loud as any of the kids, and maybe I'll be able
to surprise him backstage afterwards if I'm

lucky. There's got to be something else I could do for him though...

"Zoe! Come in, dear, he's just in the front room," Alex's mum ushers me in, before asking if I'd like a coffee.

"Okay, yes please, Mrs..."

"Sandra, please dear, I've told you before."

She is really friendly towards me, but for some reason I'm still a bit afraid of her. Could be my first impression, when she seemed a bit stiff; or it could be the fear that, like my mother, she's got some sort of Mother's Radar that knows everything. No, that can't be possible. If she did, she wouldn't have let me in the house after what we got up to last time I was here. And using her shower gel as well.

He's sitting in the front room talking to his grandmother, a lovely old lady whom I met at Alex's cousin's party back in October.

"Happy birthday!" I say, giving him a chaste, innocent kiss: on the mouth (I am his girlfriend, after all) but definitely no sexual overtones. A PG-rated kiss. I give him his present and card, which he starts to open.

The card is a fairly ordinary one with the

number 18 on it in big, glittery letters. Inside I've just wished him a happy birthday and signed it with our special code. There were lots of other things I could have written, but I remembered in time that it would have to spend a few days on his parents' mantelpiece. Then he opens the present.

I hope he likes it. He doesn't actually wear any jewellery at the moment, and right now is the precise time my brain realises that could be because he doesn't want to. Or maybe he just hasn't found the right thing to wear yet.

Looks like I have, though. He takes it out of the box and holds it up. "That's ace, Zo. Mum, Nanna, look! Zoe got me a Cyrillic letter on a chain!"

What does he mean, Cyrillic? That's proper white gold, or at least it should be for what it cost. I hope I haven't been conned.

His grandmother looks at it, then at me and says, "Моя дорогая девочка."

Oh shit. What does this mean? I haven't gone and bought him a pendant that says, "Tell your granny to fuck off" in one single letter, have I?

Sandra can see I'm looking confused. "She's saying, 'My dear girl'. My mother came over here from St Petersburg when she was a child, in the late 1940s. That's why I've always been so fascinated with Russia. That pendant's a lovely idea, but I'm surprised you knew. Alexei doesn't exactly embrace his roots, let's say."

Alex's grandmother smiles.

"Of course I do speak English as you know, my dear, but when I saw you'd gone to the trouble of finding that pendant, and the fact that Alexei must be quite important to you, I slipped back into the mother tongue."

The she says something else: "Если она умеет готовить , то ему придется выйти замуж за этого один" and starts laughing.

Come on, Sandra, help us out. What does that mean, then?

Mrs Ryan giggles and looks at Alex as if she's wary of his reaction.

"She said, 'If she can cook as well, he'll have to marry this one'."

At this point, Alex is turning purple and the heat in my cheeks suggests I'm the same. Then, he decides to throw in a real curveball:

"Zoe's great in the kitchen, actually," he says, looking at me with a knowing smile.

What? I've done a few things for him in the kitchen, but food didn't have much to do with it.

"You know those long doughnuts with cream in? She did one of them for me last week."

At this, point, I have to put my hand over my mouth to stop myself laughing and giving the game away. In fact, I think Mr Ryan might even be on to us, because he says, winking, "Ooh, Zoe, sounds great. Maybe you could give my Sandra a few tips."

This is too much. I decide it's probably time I went. He comes to the door to see me out.

 "Sorry about that. My nan's lovely, but she can be a nightmare sometimes."

"Your nan wasn't the problem, not as much as you nearly telling them what we got up to last week!"

He smiles that smile, and raises his eyebrows. "Hey, I just liked the doughnut you gave me. What's wrong with that?"

I squeeze his hand.

"Hmm. And I nearly died when your nan mentioned getting married!"

However, for some reason I can't tell you, it's certainly nothing connected to my brain, I continue, "But... it wouldn't be that bad, would it? As long as we never ran out of squirty cream and shower gel?"

He seems a bit stunned by that, and changes the subject. I'm a total idiot.

"Erm, suppose so. Hey, thanks again for the chain. They told us we're not allowed to wear things like that during the performances, but any other time, I'm never going to take it off. Ever."

The little voice in my head that provides the common sense, usually just after I've spoken, isn't very happy with me right now: Oh my God, Zoe, what the fuck have you just said? We only just got over the Love hurdle, and you've gone and mentioned marriage? He's going to think he's with a right bunny boiler now. I should just shut up. Still, looks like he's just ignoring that comment. Probably for the best.

I wish him luck for the show, still not letting on that I'll be there, give him a kiss (a lot less innocent than the last one because no-one's watching) and head back home until tonight.

CHAPTER 12

"I'm looking forward to seeing Alex actually doing a bit of acting," Kate says, as we take our seats.

"Well, this isn't exactly going to be Shakespeare, he is only in the chorus," I point out, as if I'm apologising for him in advance. I mean, I know he's brilliant, and obviously he's been chosen as the lead chorus member, but what if my friends think he's rubbish? It's like when you show someone a YouTube clip, telling them it's going to be hilarious and they're going to die laughing, and they don't think it's funny at all.

"Does he sing at all?" Jay asks. "That's what I want to see."

He does sing, mostly as part of a group, but

he does get to do two solo lines – and with the star of the show, which is even better because more people will notice him. It's 'Cinderella', and in the title role is Kellie Ashton from the soap, 'Croft Estate'. She's 23 and the soap's biggest star at the moment, but she signed up for this panto much earlier in the year when she was only a new cast member and there was no indication of how popular she'd be with the viewing public. It's turned out to be a bit of a stroke of luck for the theatre, with sold-out performances every night.

The curtains go up, and there's a huge round of applause when Kellie comes on, dressed as the pre-transformation Cinders. A few wolf whistles echo round the auditorium as well – she's a dead cert to win 'Sexiest Female' at the next Soap Awards. Whatever. I'm just waiting to see the real star of this show. And to see his face when I surprise him.

When I went to the panto he was in last year, there was a part where they stopped the story for a few minutes, and one of the characters read out some birthday greetings to people in the audience. That got me thinking: when they do that, perhaps they could mention it was Alex's birthday too? I know I can't do much, but it'd be one way of marking the day for him – a whole theatre of people wishing him a happy birthday. That's got to be something an actor like him would love.

So, earlier this afternoon, I rang the theatre and explained the situation. When I was put through to the floor manager, they said they'd be happy to do it, especially as it was his 18th. They even said I'd be able to pop backstage after the show to see him briefly. It's all in place. All I have to do now is wait.

The show is pretty enjoyable, even for three cynical teenagers like us. Alex is fab at everything: dancing, walking onto the stage with a pumpkin and of course, he steals the show with his two lines in Kellie Ashton's song - well, as far as I'm concerned, anyway. He's definitely a better singer than her. Then it's time for the birthday shout-outs.

The Fairy Godmother takes centre stage and asks us to clap for a boy who's five tomorrow, twin girls who were eight yesterday and a lady who's not celebrating her birthday, but she's ninety-five and has never been to a pantomime before. Then, she lifts her wand and says,

"And we've got one more, very special shout-out for one of the boys, or should I say, a young man in our chorus... Alex! Is Alex there?"

There's about a minute's wait while the

message gets to Alex and he comes onto the stage. Just as when he introduced me to his parents, for an actor he can appear unusually shy sometimes.

"This is Alex," the Fairy Godmother says, somewhat unnecessarily, "and it's a special day for him because he's 18 today... and the poor lad's spending his first night as an adult with you lot."

A huge, exaggerated, "Ahhhh!" reverberates around the theatre.

"So can we give him a big round of applause?"

The audience comply immediately. A little girl, possibly the youngest member of the chorus because she's so tiny, comes onto the stage and gives Alex a bottle of Champagne with a large gold bow on it.

"Have a fantastic birthday Alex, from all of us at 'Cinderella'. Can we have one more round of applause for everyone who's got a birthday today?"

Another round of applause, while Alex leaves the stage and the actors resume their positions, ready to continue the show.

I hope he enjoyed his surprise. The Champagne was nice of them, I didn't expect that. I settle back into my seat to watch the rest of the show, but all I can think about is seeing him backstage at the end of it.

Once the show's over and the theatre's emptying out, I approach a member of staff and mention that the manager had said I could go backstage. After a quick conversation on the two-way radio they have clipped to their uniform, they show me to where the chorus members are almost all in their stage academy uniform of jogging bottoms and hoodies, wiping off makeup.

"Zo!" he says, actually whisking me off the floor a little in a flamboyant hug. "Thank you. I felt a bit of a div, but thanks for doing that for me."

"Well, I haven't been able to do anything else for you today, have I? I just wanted to make today something you'd always remember."

"You've certainly done that," he says, as we both notice Kellie Ashton enter the room.

Obviously, he's been rehearsing and acting with her for a few weeks now, but you can still see he's in awe of this person who's where he wants to be. Or it just because she's totally gorgeous? Okay, she's wearing Ugg boots, leggings and a T shirt now, but her calendar's in all the shops for Christmas. Everyone in the country's seen how amazing she looks in a bikini.

"Hey, birthday boy!" she calls to him, "Why didn't you say anything? And is this Zoe?" She turns to me. "Aren't you just the world's best girlfriend?"

She's being perfectly charming to me, but I feel a bit unsettled by this impossibly good-looking woman paying this much attention to my boyfriend. If she wanted to take him from me, I couldn't even begin to compete. She's gorgeous, famous and probably rich as well.

It's not even any good thinking, what would she want with a lowly chorus boy? I know exactly what she'd want with him, because it's what I want with him and haven't been able to have much of for the last four weeks because he's been rehearsing. With her.

"Zoe, I've been working with your boyfriend for a while now, and I've got to tell you something: I want him."

What? The bitch is being as brazen as this? Can't you go off and find yourself some footballer or something? Someone your own age? I look at Alex. If any of the things he's said to me have meant anything, he's going to have to prove it now.

He's just standing there, looking really confused.

Kellie Ashton goes on, smiling as if I should be delighted she's about to steal my boyfriend.

"You see, we need to recast the character of Jake Hartley in 'Croft Estate', and I'm going to tell the casting director about Alex. I think he'd be perfect, and the viewers would just love him."

I sigh with relief. She really had me going there... then the reality of what she's said hits both of us. A part in a soap? Not just a week-long accessory to a storyline, but an actual character? I look at Alex. His face is twitching with excitement, and still some confusion.

"Hang on, though, Kellie," he says. "I remember Jake Hartley. Last time he was in the show, before he went to live in America with his dad, wasn't he blond with blue eyes? And wouldn't he still only be about fourteen by now?"

Kellie laughs. "Yes, he was, but casting directors never pay any attention to that, do they? I mean, look at my sister in the show."

True enough, I think. Kellie's character has a sister, who went into a coma as a short redhead and came out of it as a tall blonde.

"Once they've seen you, Alex, they won't want anyone else. I know it."

Err, alright love, I think. You've been very helpful, but keep your distance. I'm still not 100% convinced her motives are pure. Still, my Alex is going to get his big break! Whether she's got her eye on him for strictly professional reasons or not, Kellie's right: there is no way anyone else is going to get this part.

My phone buzzes. It's Jay, who's been waiting in the multi-storey a couple of roads away, telling me if we want a lift home, he's going in five minutes. It'd be impossible to get a taxi before midnight, so I ask Alex if he's ready to go.

"Almost," he says, reaching for his rucksack. "Just one more thing and I'm done."

He finds the chain I gave him in the side compartment of the bag.

"Put this on for me," he whispers. "I haven't felt right without it."

I fasten it around his neck, and we look into each others' eyes for a second. It's not like other times. I'm not getting a racing heart or the throbbing feeling in my knickers that I usually feel when all I want is a hot, hard shag. In fact, I don't feel like there's anything sexy about this moment. Instead, I just want to take my boyfriend - no, my man – home so I can make love to him. I want him to look back on this night and know he was loved.

Kate's already in the front seat of the car, so Alex and I get in the back. It's only a short journey to my house, but I find it impossible to keep from leaning across and giving him a few kisses, ignoring the complaints of "Ewww, get a room, you two!" coming from the front.

It's pretty dark in the back of the car, and I think about stroking his groin to give him a taste of what he can expect when we get home, but instead I just take his hand and put my head on his shoulder. He leans his head towards mine, kissing my hair.

On my doorstep, I reach for my keys and tell him, "Whatever you want tonight, I'll do it. For you. I want to give you a night you'll never forget."

He puts the bottle of Champagne on the floor, then takes my hands, holding them at hip level. Why has his face dropped? What's he going to say?

"Babe, I'm really sorry, but would you mind if I just went home? I'm shattered." He pauses, a bit embarrassed. "Maybe how busy the last week's been has taken it out of me a bit. I'm not sure I'd be any use to you if I came in."

This is not how tonight was supposed to play out. I'd bought a bottle of wine and a little box of expensive chocolates. I'd been planning on feeding them to him, sitting on the couch, before taking him upstairs to touch, stroke and kiss every part of him in what I hoped would be a sensual, loving experience. Suppose there's no point telling him I haven't been wearing any knickers since I slipped them off in the toilets at the theatre, just before I surprised him backstage.

"I just wanted to make tonight special for you," I say, with obvious disappointment in my voice.

"Babe, you have, you have. I love my chain and it was great when they gave me that round of applause."

Not as good as Kellie bloody Ashton and her offer of a part in 'Croft Estate', I find myself thinking. I know I'm being unfair, it's great of her to offer to help him, but I can't help thinking that when he does look back on this day, the best thing that happened to him on his eighteenth birthday won't have had anything to do with me.

"And you're going to be in a soap, properly!" I

say, as cheerily as I can manage, because it is a pretty great thing for him.

"There's no certainty of that," he says. "Kellie's going to put a word in, that's all. They might take one look at me and hate me."

Huh, like that's going to happen.

"Look, babe. I really need to get some sleep, but what about Christmas Eve? I've got the day off because there's no performance. They have to let the main actors get home for a day to see their families. So, I'll be all yours."

"I'll hold you to that," I say, holding him close and giving him a long kiss. "Happy birthday, Alex. I love you."

He tells me he loves me too, then he's gone; leaving me disappointed, alone and acutely aware of a draught blowing up my skirt.

CHAPTER 13

When I was a small child, Christmas Eve always seemed to be about three times longer than any other day of the year. It seemed that my mum would be spending all day cleaning, and no matter where I was, I was in the way. Meanwhile, I would spend all day wondering when it was time to get a bath. I usually got a bath before heading to bed, and my five-year-old mind must have reasoned that getting a bath, and putting on the new pyjamas I always got for this night, was the only way I had of bringing Christmas Day a bit closer. I think I got my 'evening bath' at about 1pm one year, I was so excited.

Then, when I was about thirteen or fourteen, I really found Christmas boring: I'd long stopped believing in the idea of whether or not Santa would come, I wasn't lying awake wondering if I'd got what I asked for, since most of the time I'd gone to the shops with Mum and picked it out myself, and yet I couldn't do any of the things that are part of an adult Christmas, like having a drink and going out clubbing.

This year, though, I don't think I've looked forward to it more. Now I've got my Alex. We can't actually see each other on the day itself because we'll both be visiting relatives, so our special day is going to be Christmas Eve. Today.

Mum went out at nine this morning, to do the last bits of shopping, then she's going to spend the afternoon on a bit of a personal tradition, visiting her grandparents' and aunties' graves and putting some flowers on them. It's always seemed a bit gloomy to me, doing something like that at what's supposed to be a happy time of year, but she'd just say Christmas is about family, and we've agreed to leave it there.

Because she'll be busy with that all day and won't be home 'til about four, I've got the job of giving the house a final clean. I decide to get the job done before Alex is due round at about eleven, so by half past ten, the house is tidy. Just me who needs to get ready now.

After a shower, I wonder what to wear. I consider going with his favourite, the black dress with the red roses, the one from our first night and Halloween, then I think that might be a bit much, especially when he'll probably just have jeans and a T-shirt on. In the end, I decide to wear a sexy maroon red bra and knickers set (I've got quite a few these days, it's more fun buying them if you've got an appreciative audience) under my satin dressing gown. Nothing else.

Those posh chocolates are on a little plate on the coffee table, upon which I've strewn a few rose petals. The bottle of Champagne he left behind the other night is in the fridge. There's even a jar of Nutella hidden under my bed for if we fancy trying a variation on the squirty cream experience.

I'm really going for it, but to be honest, I'm not sure what 'it' will end up being. I mean, that time I went to his house a couple of weeks ago, I knew I wanted sex: hard, fast, leave-you-breathless sex... but then on his birthday, I was hoping for something softer, more meaningful and loving. Who knows what's going to happen today?

The doorbell rings. Time to find out, I guess.

"Parcel for Thompson? Your mum not in,

love?"

Oh. There's a delivery driver with a large box on the doorstep. What's Mum gone and bought this time? This guy's been to our house lots of times since Mum developed her shopping channel habit. I feel really self-conscious, trying to sign for the parcel without letting my dressing gown either fall open at the top, or blow up at the bottom. I know my bra-strap's on show, but if I try to cover it up, I'm afraid I'll end up showing something much worse.

As I'm handing the back the electronic pad, Alex arrives. He eyes me up and down. He's impressed.

The delivery man looks at him, then at me, and says, "That's everything. Well, you have a good day, now" - and did he just wink?

Once I've shut the door, Alex hangs up his jacket and sits down in the middle of the couch. I offer him a glass of the Champagne and sit at one end with my legs draped across his. We sit and talk about what we've been up while we've been apart from each other: he tells me that Kellie Ashton won't be speaking to the casting director until after New Year, last night's performance nearly had to be stopped for a bit in the middle when Buttons fell over and sprained his ankle, and about how he's going to be spending Christmas Day itself at his grandparents' house, where after a few vodkas his nan will usually start singing the Russian national anthem during the queen's speech.

I don't have much to tell him; I'm just enjoying his company. It doesn't have to be red-hot sex all the time: this, just sitting together, being close to each other, is all I need right now. I feel safe, warm and slightly numbed from the alcohol. I wish we could spend Christmas Day together, but there'll be loads of other times when we will.

Ooh, look. I said it again.

After a couple of glasses of the fizz, we both decide we're not really very keen on it, so we stick the glasses on the drainer and return to the couch, where he selects one of the chocolates, places it to my lips and I nibble at it lightly. Having bitten off one side of the square, I stick my finger inside and dot the sugary fondant centre onto the end of his nose before licking it off. He laughs.

"Oh, right, if you're going to do that, it's war!"

He picks up another chocolate and breaks it open with his teeth, then pulls my dressing gown open a little. He then smears what looks like a raspberry centre down the middle of my chest. Next, he playfully pushes me back onto the couch, taking my arms by the wrists and holding me down by them, above my head.

I think my soft centre's melting.

He leans over me and removes the raspberry filling from my cleavage with a few intense licks. He releases my hands so I can sit up again, and he reaches for another one. The long, thin one, I think it's called a baton. He places the tip of it into his mouth, then edges towards me with the other end pointing out. I nibble at the other end until we meet in a dark chocolate-flavoured kiss, our tongues tasting the bittersweet cocoa and each other.

After the chocolate has gone, we continue the kiss. I move back so that I'm lying on the couch and he positions himself on top of me. I can feel he's getting hard through his jeans. My dressing gown's slipped open at the front, so he's touching my skin. Suddenly, he jerks up and moves away slightly.

"Are you okay?" I ask him. "We can just cuddle and talk some more if you don't feel like it."

"Oh no, I definitely want to."

Thank God for that, I think to myself. The

other night I could understand, but if it happened twice running I'd start to get worried. He looks down at where I'm still lying on the couch and smiles.

"I just think we should take our time. This is a special day. This is our Christmas and I want everything to be perfect." He stands up, and extends his hand to me, just as he did on our first night.

"Let's go up to bed, babe. I'm going to give you everything you want."

I stand up, and we share one last kiss before he leads me up the stairs.

Earlier on, I thought I'd try to make my room look a bit more special: more of those rose petals, all over the duvet cover, and the curtains are closed even though it's the middle of the day. I put a flame-free oil burner on before he arrived so it smells gorgeous, and the room is glowing a range of different colours from fairy lights I've placed along the picture rails and around my bedpost. As he enters the room, I ask him what he thinks.

"Babe, it's like we've got our own beautiful little Christmas grotto. It's amazing."

We come together and kiss again, and I know this is going to be perfect: he wants to please me, and I want to do anything I can to make this special for him. This isn't going to be one of those fast, hard, breathless shags... this time, it's all about the love.

I undo my dressing gown and let it slip to the floor. Then, I step towards him, and pull his T-shirt up and over his head. Neither of us speak, but I can see he's enjoying the idea of me undressing him. Next, I reach for his belt buckle. It's surprisingly tricky to undo a belt you aren't wearing, but I get it undone and he steps out of his jeans. Eventually, he's just wearing his underpants. And the pendant, of course. That stays on.

I take both of his hands and walk backwards to my bed. We both climb on and lie sideways, looking in towards each other. After a minute or two of us both looking at each other nervously, as if we were a couple of strangers, he reaches across, places his arm around my waist and pulls me towards him. I lift my leg up at the knee so it crosses his body. We're so close, but we still have the barrier of our underwear. It feels even more sensual than being naked.

Then we kiss, rocking back and forth gently. His erection is touching the gusset of my knickers, which are pretty moist already. I look at him. "Do you want...?"

"No, not yet," he whispers, continuing to rock me. "I don't want to stop this, this is just..."

Another slow, tantalising kiss. I'm so turned on, when we actually do start having sex, I'm going to be done in a second, I know it.

After a few more minutes of gentle rocking, I pull away and press him onto his back. I straddle him. I want to slide him inside me right now, but as he says, we've got all the time in the world to make our first Christmas unforgettable.

I run my mouth along his body, teasing him with soft, fluttery kisses, brushing his skin with my eyelashes as I move. Then it's time to slide off his undies. I put my hands in at the sides, he lifts his bum a little and I pull them down. His penis is huge and standing up against his body. I take it in my hands carefully, running my fingers up and down it to arouse him even more.

"Tell me what you want, " I tease him, still stroking.

"Oh, you know what I want," he says, almost in a whisper.

"But I want you to tell me," I say, waiting only a second for his answer. I don't want to torture him, just make him wait and anticipate the sensation.

Slowly, I slide the full length of his penis into my mouth and start moving my head up and down. I spend several minutes sucking, flicking my tongue around the head and stroking the bottom until he groans and touches my head – our signal that if I don't want him to go off in my mouth, it's time to stop.

"Oh my God," he says quietly. "I am just so turned on right now, but I've got to do something for you. I've got to make you feel as incredible as you just made me feel."

And he does. After he carefully removes my knickers, he spends ages, taking the time to pleasure me in the most intimate way; deep tongue strokes that leave me almost dizzy. For a second I feel as if I've lost consciousness, but as I'm lying down, I'm not sure.

Eventually, he resumes his position next to me. He undoes my bra and starts kissing my boobs, but I lift his head up to meet mine and say, "You said you'll give me whatever I want. The only thing I want is to know you love me. Nothing else matters."

"Oh, I love you," he whispers, sitting up and taking me by the hands so that I do the same. "I know what we should do."

He arranges my legs so that I'm facing him, but sitting astride him. I have to use my hands to slide him inside, but from this angle he feels even bigger than usual. Once he's in, we start rocking again. It's such an intense feeling that it doesn't take either of us long until we both explode with excitement and love. We stay in the upright embrace for a few minutes afterwards.

We lie back on the bed holding each other closely afterwards, then after a while, I realise he's fallen asleep. My poor love, he's been working so hard, and well... I did just take it out of him a bit. I don't mind. In fact, I love that he feels so relaxed and secure with me.

I nip downstairs, pour myself a glass of wine and sit beside him in bed as he sleeps, lazily picking rose petals out of his hair. This has been the perfect Christmas Eve. I've got everything I want.

CHAPTER 14

January's been a busy month. So much seems
to have happened in the last few weeks.

Christmas Day itself was a bit dull after the
amazing time we'd had the day before, but we
spoke on the phone. He loved the aftershave,
and I still haven't taken off the gorgeous red
Murano glass heart he gave me as my present.

I spent the rest of the Christmas period
catching up with relatives and working
through the ton of coursework I had from
school. I won't say I was too busy to miss Alex,
I just knew if I couldn't see him while he was
doing two performances a day, I might as well
get my work done and keep myself occupied.

We were able to be together for New Year's
Eve, though. Again, he had the night off. His

parents invited me to spend the evening round at their house. I don't know if it's because we've been together for nearly four months, or because Alex has turned eighteen, but they're okay with the idea of me stopping over now. I have to say, I was amazed when Sandra suggested I bring an overnight bag, "Because you'll never get a taxi dear, and let's face it, we'll probably all be too plastered to run you home."

I expected to be told I'd be on the couch, but she just smiled and said, "I imagine it'll be nice for he and you to wake up together on your first New Year's Day."

That floored me on two levels: one, the acceptance of us sharing a bed, and two, her use of the word 'first'. It's not just me who thinks there'll be others.

I think my initial impression of Sandra as the mother-in-law from Hell was a bit unfair. She's always been lovely to me, and she was a lot cooler than I'd be about the Kellie Ashton calendar on display in the Ryan kitchen, signed with the message, "To Tom, lots of love, Kellie" followed by three kisses.

New Year's Eve was fun. It was strange being away from Mum; if she isn't working, we always see the New Year in together. She was

okay about it though. She just said she'd wait
up 'til midnight to get a quick call from me,
then she'd need to get some sleep because she
was on an early shift eight hours later.

The evening was spent with Alex's family,
chatting and getting a bit tipsy – the usual
things you do when you're just hanging
round, waiting for midnight. Then, when the
room was filled with the sounds of Big Ben on
the telly, followed by fireworks everywhere,
Alex and I had our first kiss of the new year.

"Happy New Year, babe," he said, smiling at
me. "Who knows where it's going to take us?"

"Yeah," I said, because I couldn't think of
anything else to reply.

I know where this year's going to take him,
anyway, I remember thinking. Down to
London, where they film 'Croft Estate'.

Kellie Ashton was as good as her word. In the
first week of January, Alex was summoned to
London to see one of the casting directors,
who'd seen some photos of him (his parents
took him to a professional photographer last
year and got some made up. I've got one in a
frame on my bedside table) and,
unsurprisingly, wanted to meet him

immediately. That meeting went well and he's got another appointment down there to do a read-through with the actor who'd be playing his father. If that goes well, then the part could be his.

This is exactly what he's always wanted: a proper acting job. It's what I knew he wanted to do when I met him, before I was with him – so why do I feel so miserable about this? If I love him, shouldn't I be happier about this?

I'm just so afraid this'll be the end for us. We're having a great time together at the moment; I love him more than I ever thought I could love anyone, and he tells me he loves me all the time.

But does he love me more than achieving his dream? And do I love him enough to let him go?

CHAPTER 15

I guess the best thing about this month is that
the panto season finally ended. I got him back
on January 4th, and after he had a couple of
nights to catch up on his sleep, we've been
shagging like we're an endangered species
every time we can be alone together. It was
only when I got him back that I realised how
much I missed him.

Tonight Alex's parents are officially celebrating
his birthday, since we couldn't really do it at
the time. They've booked at table at Le Bistro,
and I've been invited as well. That really
makes me feel like they're accepting me as a
permanent fixture in their son's life, not just
someone he's hanging around with for now.

We have a lovely evening. It's nice for us to do
things like this together; for the last six weeks

it's felt like we've had so little time together, it's just been about arranging the odd times to meet up, where we did nothing but have sex. Now I've got him back, I'm looking forward to things like going to the cinema with him or just wandering round town on a Saturday again.

When we get back to his house, we sit downstairs with his parents and have a last drink while Leo goes up to bed. I can see Alex is looking at me, his eyes rolling up in the direction of the stairs. I get the hint, and anyway, it is fairly late.

"Tell you what, Sandra, Tom. I'm shattered. Thanks for inviting me, but I think I'll head up now."

Without even the slightest attempt to be subtle about it, Alex springs up and affects a yawn.

"Yeah, I'm worn out as well. See you in the morning. Thanks again for tonight."

It takes us less than five minutes to brush our teeth and curl up in bed together. We know his parents are still awake, and Leo could be, we haven't checked, so there's only one thing for it: silent sex.

I wasn't sure it'd be for me, but if we don't

want anyone to hear us, there's no choice. As it turns out it's... just gorgeous, if a little difficult to keep quiet. All the usual tongue-teasing, stroking and gentle rocking (that's a definite favourite, it turns us both on so much), but the added excitement of having to keep silent when you want to moan or scream. Like it's our little secret.

At the end, we're both shivering with the intensity and intimacy of our silent, secret love... I know, who am I kidding? It's hardly as though his parents think we've gone up together for a game of cards, is it? Even though we're both finished, we kiss for a few moments with him still inside me. Even when he's losing the hardness, it's still a lovely feeling.

Eventually he removes himself and takes off the condom. Then he turns on his bedside lamp and looks at it. What's on earth's he doing?

"Shit, Zo. This condom's spilt. My finger went through it when I took it off."

As he drops it to the floor beside his bed, I'm aware of a sensation I've never had before, and to be honest, it's not a particularly pleasant one. The sheet underneath me feels all damp, and I can feel something trickling out of me.

Ugh. Guess this is what they mean by sleeping in the wet patch.

Still, that's not exactly going to be a massive concern right now. How do you sleep when you might have just got pregnant?

Oh fuck. This can't be happening.

This is a nightmare. I can't be pregnant, I just can't. For so many reasons.

Alex has got his reading coming up, and he's going to get the part and be in 'Croft Estate'... the last thing he needs right now is a pregnant girlfriend screwing things up. His parents will think I've done it on purpose, to trap him.

And never mind him, what about me? I might not be 100% sure what I want to do career-wise, but being stuck with a baby at the age of eighteen definitely isn't in the plan. I'd be useless with a baby anyway, I don't think I've ever even held one. What's nine months from now? It'd be October. I want to be starting uni then, not going to a bloody ante-natal class.

Why did that stupid condom have to split on us? We've been doing it for months without a single problem. Why did this have to happen?

It's 3am now, and I'm still in a panic. We've spent the time since the condom split checking how and where to get the Morning-after Pill on our phones. It's a relief to see that it can be taken for up to seventy-two hours after, because basically, his swimmers have to take a bit of time to nose about and see if there's an egg around. Obviously, I already knew how the process worked, I just didn't realise it potentially took several days to happen. He switches his phone off and lies back down.

"So, you're not actually pregnant at this moment," he says, with some relief.

"Yeah, but I might be tomorrow if we don't do something. It doesn't mean it's all okay."

"I know that, babe. But at least it means we're not getting rid of a baby. We're just making sure there never is any baby."

I have to admit, that makes me feel a little better, too. We're not terminating anything, we're just stopping it from being created, which is the same as what we do with the condoms anyway.

First thing in the morning we're going to go and get the Pill. I'm up for going right now and finding an all-night pharmacy, the website we looked at says that it works best if you take it within the first twelve hours after sex. The only reason I don't is that his parents might wake and wonder what we were up to.

I never thought I'd ever need to take the Morning-after Pill. I'll admit, I always thought it was for girls who were a bit stupid and just shagged anyone without being with them properly.

Fair enough, point taken.

As I've always said, I did know Alex for a year before we had sex, he just became my boyfriend after the event. Slightly the wrong way round, but it's worked out so far. Even so, I don't think either of us is ready to play Mummies and Daddies yet. No, there's no way we can even consider this. As soon as it's light enough to go the chemist, we're going.

At eight o'clock, we both get dressed. I'd brought some jeans and a top to wear to go home in, when I thought our Saturday morning might be spent curled up in bed, wrapped up in each other. Before this happened.

We have a coffee, but neither of us can face the idea of breakfast. Alex makes some lame joke about morning sickness and for the first time since the Monday after we got together, I'm annoyed with him. I'm really not in the mood for jokes, and besides, someone might hear him.

We're at the chemist before it's open. When the pharmacist arrives, she smiles and tells us to take a seat while she turns on all the lights and the till. She doesn't even ask why we're here. I guess we're not the first terrified couple she's had to help out.

When she's ready, she asks which one of us needs help.

I stammer, "Well, it's me, last night we, well I need the Morning-after Pill."

She remains calm. This is obviously nothing new to her. She directs me to a semi-open cubicle, asking if I want Alex to stay outside.

"Perhaps if he'd done that last night," I say, with a nervous laugh. He gives me a smile. Now I'm here and I know we're going to sort this out, I'm getting my sense of humour back a little.

"Can I come in, Zo? You shouldn't have to do this on your own."

The pharmacist smiles, like she thinks this is really sweet.

"It's unusual to get a couple here, actually. Usually it's just the woman."

Woman? What woman? I feel like a frightened little girl.

The pharmacist, who introduces herself as Lisa, asks us what happened. We tell her how we did use contraception (I don't want her to think we're a pair of idiots) but it broke, and how we need to avoid a pregnancy.

Lisa asks when my last period was, and when I tell her it was about ten days ago, her eyebrows rise a little.

"Right. Sometimes, if you're due on or just finished, there's less of a risk. Even then, we don't advise that people leave it to chance. So in your case, I'm definitely going to give you the Pill. There's a strong chance you would become pregnant without it."

I feel even more sick than I did before now. It sounds like the clock's ticking and I'm only hours away from it happening. I just want to get the Pill, take it and go home.

Seeming to read my mind, or again, probably because she's seen a lot of girls like me, Lisa fetches a plastic cup of water.

"Would you like to take it now, before you go home? You can leave the packaging in our bin here if you'd be afraid of your parents finding it. I'll still give you the information booklet."

"Sooner the better," I say, popping the Pill out of its blister pack and swallowing it. It's quarter past nine, and I reckon we had sex at about midnight, so we're within the twelve-hour optimum time.

"And that's it, you're done," Lisa reassures us. Have you got anything strenuous planned for the rest of today? If so, it might be better to give it a miss and relax if you can. Some of the side effects I've discussed with you might make you feel a bit low today."

"Thanks. No, I think this has just changed my plans a bit. I think I'll just go home and get some sleep."

While we're paying for the Pill (you can get it for free in some places, but they weren't open yet and we reckoned it was worth £25 to get it done as soon as possible), I catch sight of myself in a mirror on a shelf behind the counter. God, I look rough. Probably because we've been up all night worrying, and I feel a bit hungover after last night as well. A quiet day at home relaxing is definitely what I need.

We head back to his house to get my bags, and he persuades me to eat some toast. I'm still a bit nervous. What if it doesn't work and I get pregnant anyway? There's always stories in my mum's magazines along the lines of 'My

Miracle Baby' and 'I Was On The Pill... Now
I've Got Twins!' Knowing my luck, our baby'd
be some contraception-defying force of nature.

Our baby. I wonder if it'd have had his eyes.

Alex offers to walk me home, even though it's
broad daylight. When we arrive at my door, he
gives me a tight hug.

"Are you sure you'll be okay, babe? I don't
want to leave you."

"I'll be fine. There's nothing you can do,
anyway. We've just got to wait for it to start
working. I'll just have a quiet afternoon
watching telly or something."

"Okay. Just call me if you need anything." He
kisses me warmly, then leaves.

Inside, I make myself another coffee and
change into my pyjamas. I just want to go to
bed and sleep, forget this ever happened... if I
can.

I sleep until about three o'clock, when I wake
up to find myself bleeding and with really sore
boobs. The leaflet in the tablet packaging said
this would probably happen. I'm relieved,
actually. At least I know the Pill's having an
effect. Hopefully we're going to get away with it
this time.

I lie in bed, watching TV. I feel bloated and a bit tearful. I don't know if it's caused by whatever's in the Pill or what, but a thought enters my head. I know it never existed, but the thought of the baby Alex and I might have had is something I just can't get out of my mind. It'd definitely have had his beautiful eyes; dark hair, soft skin and a cute little smile. I wonder what name we could have given him?

No! Stop. These are not thoughts you can have. Get them out of your head. You've only been with him four and a half months. He's got his career, you're going to have yours. You're both too young. Babies are just not on the list of things to do.

It must just be the hormones or whatever they put in the Pill making me a bit crazy. I wasn't thinking of babies before last night, why am I doing it now?

I go downstairs and make some dinner for Mum because she's due home at six, but I don't really want anything. I'm feeling pretty nauseous. Again, I take this as a good sign.

When Mum comes home, I tell her I'm feeling rough, but don't let her know why. I just don't know what she'd say: I told you to be careful, I knew this'd happen eventually... whatever it'd be, I'm really not in the mood for it. I eat a few mouthfuls of the meal I made before heading back upstairs to continue moping and hopefully, not get pregnant.

At around half past seven, Alex pokes his head round the door.

"Your mum said it was okay to come up." He's got a big bag of Revels and a bottle of wine. "Thought you could do with some company. To be honest, I've been thinking about you all day. I only didn't text because I didn't want to disturb you if you were asleep. I brought you these."

"Oh, that's sweet of you," I say, as he kisses my cheek. "I can't have any alcohol tonight, though. It said it was best to avoid it, so I'm taking that as an order. Maybe I should lay off the chocolate as well, I feel fat enough already."

"Don't be daft, babe. That's just the side effects." He was up reading those websites with me in the early hours, so he knows exactly what's happening to me. "You're still as gorgeous as ever. Here, have a flat one."

He opens the bag of sweets and puts a Galaxy counter into my mouth. I shift to the other side of the bed to make room for him as he sits next to me.

We sit on my bed and watch some brainless Saturday night TV which helps take our minds off the events of the day and how crappy I'm feeling. Then, during the ad break, there's an advert for baby formula. A mother holds her baby while the syrupy voice over goes on about how it's the strongest bond in the world. All of the thoughts I'd banished over the afternoon come back to me.

The tears well up in my eyes. I don't wipe them away because if he sees my hand wiping my eyes, he'll know I'm crying. Eventually they overflow and run down my cheeks. Once he's seen that, there's no point trying to pretend anymore. I let out a loud sob.

"Babe? What's wrong, tell me," he turns to hold me. He sighs as he realises.

"You're thinking about what it would have been like, aren't you?"

"No," I lie. "I think my hormones are just all over the place. I mean, maybe I was going to be pregnant, then I take a tablet with stuff in it to stop me being pregnant; I'm just all messed up."

At this point I stop speaking, which is probably for the best considering I'm making no sense whatsoever, and just descend into whimpering into his chest like an idiot.

"Shh, don't get upset, babe," he says, holding me close and rubbing my head gently through my hair. "I don't think what you're feeling is weird at all."

He stops stroking my hair.

"You're going to think I'm mad when I tell you this, but I've spent a lot of today thinking about it as well. I ended up imagining us with a baby girl. She was so lovely, just like you with your cute chocolate button eyes."

I look up at him in complete shock. His eyes are welling up too. I can't believe this. Since he's been so honest, I have to tell him the truth.

"In my mind it was a little boy. Just like his dad."

He kisses me and squeezes my hand.

"Well, there's only thing for it, isn't there? I guess we'll just have to have one of each. One day."

"Are you serious?" I have to twist my head to look him in the eye.

"Totally serious." He kisses my forehead. "I'd love for us to have kids. Just not now. In a few years, when I've managed to make enough money to look after you."

I should get annoyed at that. I don't need a man to look after me, I can look after myself, I should say to him... but right now, the idea of him wanting to take care of me, and of the child he wants to have with me, sounds so lovely I can't say anything.

Another tear runs down my cheek. I slide down the bed a little so I can rest my head on his chest. It's been a tough day, but I know one thing: now's clearly not the right time, but we're going to have a baby. We'll be a family.

And, after everything he's done today, I know he wouldn't leave us.

CHAPTER 16

It's been two months since I passed my driving test, and I'm starting to worry I'm going to forget everything I learned. Since I stopped having my weekly lessons, the only driving I've been able to do is when Jay's let me have a go in his car a couple of times. We can't go onto any roads because I'm not insured, but the driveway and front of Jay's house are as big as some roads anyway, so that doesn't matter.

I haven't been able to do any driving apart from that, and as for being able to buy a car – I've got some money saved, I could probably get an old banger, but it's the insurance that'll be the big expense. How can the insurance be more than the cost of the car itself? That's insane.

Things at school are okay. I still have my

lunchtime catch-ups with Kate, and Alex spends most lunchtimes with his mates. We don't want to be one of those weird couples who can't stand to be apart from each other. Anyway, when we do get together, we prefer it to be just us. He may be a natural performer, but I still feel a bit funny when he gives me a cheeky kiss in the common room.

Sasha's still being a cow. I told you how I reckon she was only interested in Alex because he's been on telly, so why is she still getting on my case about being with him? I was working in the library today and she came up to my table and sneered, "Ooh, look. The freak's on her own. Your panto clown boyfriend run off with Kellie Ashton or something?"

Oh, just fuck off, I think. I got him and you didn't. Stop crying about it.

There's are lot of things I'd like to say to her, but I know she wouldn't understand most of them. In fact, I've never replied to her nasty comments at all before. I wouldn't exactly say she's bullied me during my time at school, because I've never given a shit what she thinks of me. I just never argued back because I didn't want to get into an argument with her. But now... we've all got our limits and that annoying bitch has just found mine.

I look up from my research, smile sweetly and say in my best, breezy, patronising tone, "Wow, Sasha. Well done for finding the library. I knew you'd find it sometime before we all leave... I think the picture books are down there," pointing to the other end of the room.

Her face is like thunder.

"Don't get cocky with me just 'cause you finally got some sad panto boy to shag you," she hisses. "Ewww, I bet you do all weird stuff. Do you wear a mask? You must, it's the only way anyone could do it with you. Or a bag over your head. Do you do it in the school library like a pair of bores?"

I bite my lip and sigh. It's taking every bit of restraint I've got not to punch her face in. I just keep telling myself, don't rise to it. She wants you to flip. Just don't go mad, you're better than her.

It's impossible not to say anything at all, though. Eventually, I shut off my laptop and pick my bags up to leave.

"You know what, Sasha? Say what you like. It doesn't matter. Because I'll always know you wanted him and you couldn't have him. You might get what you want all the time, but you couldn't get Alex Ryan. I did. So nothing you say can hurt me." I pick up my stuff and leave.

I hear her behind me. "You're going to regret that, freak."

"Whatever."

When I get home after school, my Auntie Mel's car is on the drive. As I put my key in the door, I hear my Uncle Dave's voice in the living room. He often pops by on a Sunday, but today's Thursday. Oh well, maybe Mum's asked her brother to give her a hand with something. Wonder why he's not using his own car though?

When I go inside, they're both sitting having a cuppa. When I've taken off my coat and poured myself a cup of tea, Mum says she's got something to tell me. Okay... this sounds ominous. I never like this sort of thing. For a second, I wonder if a relative's died and that's why they're together. They don't seem unhappy though, so it can't be that.

It's nothing horrible at all, actually. Auntie Mel's buying a new car, and the dealers offered her such a rubbish amount in part-exchange for her old one, she suggested Mum buy it from her for my 18th birthday. She's selling it to her at below the proper price, so that counts as their present to me as well.

"So, what we really need to know, Zoe," he says, "Is this what you want? Would you be able to manage the insurance? Do you even want a car?"

Do I even want a car? Has any eighteen year old ever said no to that question?

I should be able to manage the insurance as well, from what I have saved up, especially now I won't have to pay for the actual car myself. I can't believe it! I'm going to have my own car. I can't wait for my birthday now!

I tell them that I can manage the insurance and that I'm definitely interested, and give them both a big hug. Uncle Dave gives me the keys and I go out onto the drive.

The car is a ten-year-old VW Polo. 39,000 miles, which is really low for its age. Auntie Mel works from home: she makes and sells jewellery, so she doesn't have to drive very much because most of her business comes from internet sales. Sitting in the driving seat again feels strange. I look around the dashboard to see what's different from the car I learned in.

It feels great. I love it. And it's red!

I'm not going to be able to drive it yet, until I get the insurance sorted, but that should all be done in time for my birthday next week. I'm going to be able to drive to school on my 18th. This is great!

Uncle Dave leaves the car on our drive and Mum calls him a taxi home. I reach for my phone and tell Alex the good news.

"Nice one, babe. You can drive me around to my auditions now."

"My car is not going to be your taxi!" I say, with mock annoyance. "It's going to be fab, though. Think of the places we'll be able to go."

"I'm thinking more of the things we'll be able to do," he says, more quietly. "What's the back seat like?"

"Alex Ryan, do you ever think about anything else?" I laugh, although now he mentions it, that's definitely something we've got to try.

"Not where you're concerned, babe, what can I say?" He pauses, as if he's well aware of the cringiness of what he's about to say, and wants me to understand it's a joke: "You just drive me wild."

We arrange to meet at the weekend. My birthday's a week today - February 14th, or Valentine's Day as it's known to the rest of the world. Alex tells me he wants to do something special for me this Saturday. If we go anywhere on my birthday itself, everywhere'll be packed.

I've always hated my birthday being on Valentine's Day: You get sarky comments from the postman about the number of cards you've got, like you're some kind of slag, and from those people who do buy you a card, you often get the same card two or three times because there's such a lousy selection in the shops because they shift all the birthday cards aside to make room for Valentines.

Then, if you want to go out for a meal or something, like maybe for a meal with Mum, Uncle Dave, Auntie Mel and Nan, everywhere's packed out, or they're doing a 'Valentine's Special Menu'. Let me tell you, it doesn't exactly make you feel special to sit among hordes of couples having a romantic meal, and there's you with your nan.

Let's not forget the other reason I've always hated Valentine's Day. I'm usually on my own, trying not to look too jealous when Kate shows me her card and tells me about whatever Danny got her, or what she got for him. Also, there's always some girl in your class who gets one of those massive cards that you have to put in a cardboard case, not an envelope... and don't they like to make sure everyone knows about it? I used to go to bed on my birthday each year feeling like a lonely, ugly loser.

But not any more. This year Valentine's Day can mean something.

Strange how your opinion can change. I used to hate walking past cards shops between mid-January and February, pouring scorn on the idiots wasting their money on tacky gifts and cards with sick-making verses in them. This year, I couldn't wait to choose something for him. Not one of the cheap cuddly toys from a card shop, though. I want it to be something classy; something he'll always cherish.

After almost as much aimless wandering round the shops as I did at Christmas, I chose a silver bookmark. I know that sounds a bit boring, but he does use them; or rather, in all his books from school and the script for the panto, when it sat on his bedside table, there's bits off torn-off newspaper or cardboard shoved in them to mark places. I think this'll be really useful for him. I've had it engraved with, 'To my Alex, XY,Z' and wrapped it up in a lovely box. I know he'll love it.

Right now though, it's the weekend before. I still can't drive the car yet. Hopefully I should get a cover note through from the insurers I went with by around Tuesday. I wonder what we're going to do?

I'm at home, waiting for Alex to arrive for this special day out he's planned, whatever it's going to be. He told me to make sure I was wearing flat shoes, so I guess it might be something that involves a fair bit of walking. He also said to have a few layers on, so that suggests it's something outdoors. What on earth has he planned outdoors in the middle of February?

A few minutes a later, he arrives, carrying his rucksack and saying he's already rung for a cab to arrive here before he walked round from his house. We have our usual kiss and I ask him where we're going.

"You'll see," is all I can get out of him. "Hope you're going to like it."

I've never been great with surprises. I just wish he'd hurry up and tell me. I think about insisting on knowing what it is or I won't go, but then the cab arrives. Oh well, may as well go for it. If it's something awful I can always get the cab back.

"We could have got the train, but I want to

spoil you a bit," he says.

After about a twenty minute drive, we're at... the beach.

The beach, as in where you go in the middle of summer. Today is February 9th and it's more than a little chilly. I see now why he told me to make sure I was wrapped up. The tide is out but it's choppy, with noisy waves crashing in the distance. There's not a soul around, not even any dog walkers.

It's bliss. The exact opposite to Valentine's Day madness.

He looks at me, smiling. He's relieved. I guess he knew this was a gamble and I could have hated it. Instead, he's got it spot on. A romantic walk along a deserted beach with him is the perfect birthday/Valentine idea.

"Shall we?" he says, holding up his arm for me to link mine into.

We walk along the beach for about half an hour and, yes, it is cold, but it makes me feel alive. I love the sound of the waves, the feel of the sand crunching under my boots... the boyfriend who loves me enough to think of something so special.

Suddenly, he stops. "Right, this spot'll do," he

decides, dropping his rucksack and crouching down to rummage around inside it. He finds a thick blanket and lays it down. "Sit down, babe."

He fishes out a bottle of wine, two plastic wine glasses from his Mum's barbecue set and a box of chocolate batons. God, I love him. It's all perfect.

"Gotta have a picnic on the beach," he smiles at me. "It should be Champagne, but you weren't really keen, were you?"

"Nope. I guess I'm a cheap date, lucky you," I say, as I take the glass he's just filled.

He's thought of everything. He even digs a small trench next to our blanket to make sure the wine glasses and the bottle don't fall over. We stay there for about an hour, feeling a bit warmed up by the wine. There's still no-one around, so we lie down together and hold each other.

"Alex... thanks for this. It's been so, so different. That's why I love you. You don't do the dull, predictable crap other boys do. You put some thought into it."

"Well, I knew you hated everywhere being packed out on your birthday, so I thought, what's the exact opposite of packed out?

169

Where would nobody be in February?"

We're lying on our sides, facing each other. I pick a chocolate baton out of the box to my side and we have our third chocolate baton kiss... which turns into him moving closer to me, so that our bodies are pressed together. He's got that hungry look in his eyes again. It makes me feel sexy, knowing how much he wants me. I'm not going to lie, I'm tempted to take it further, but just because no-one's around now, you never know when some dog walker might turn up. And anyway, it is pretty cold. I sit up.

"Maybe we should go now."

"Okay, but it's not time to go home yet. Let's walk along the prom."

There's a long promenade leading from the beach to some rock shops and a café. When we get to the café, it's open and there are a group of ramblers there. Good job we did just stick to a cuddle on the beach, I think. We get some chips and sit in the window, looking out at the view. I rest my head on his shoulder. I feel so happy and contented with him.

After we've eaten, he picks up our polystyrene trays and puts them in the bin. "Right, one more thing to do before we go home. Do you want to have a bit of fun?"

Holding hands, we walk a little further along the seafront. I don't think I've been here since Dad was around, so I don't know what will be next.

It's an amusement arcade, and even though it's February, it's open. To be honest, I know a lot of people would describe it as a pretty depressing sight: the five or six people who are there are clearly not on holiday. They all seem grey and downtrodden, and you get the impression that coming down here and playing on the fruit machines is the only thing they've got to do all day before slumping back to their seaside B&B temporary accommodation. There's a smell of weed in the air, and even though the place doesn't serve alcohol, a few of them seem to have been drinking.

I realise that, having necked half a bottle of wine each on the beach, we're in no position to judge. Anyway, I used to love arcades as a kid. The bright lights, trying to grab a crappy cuddly toy; I'm looking at the place as if it's Vegas.

Alex gets some change from a machine, places half of it in my hand and says, "Let's play."

The next hour passes in a flash. I'd forgotten how much fun arcades could be. I manage to knock off a huge overhang of 2p pieces on the topple machine, Alex actually grabs a toy Minion and we have a battle to the death on 'Time Crisis' - or it would have been if I wasn't totally rubbish at computer games.

When it's time to go home, he's willing to treat me to another taxi, but I say I don't mind getting the train. We sit together - with his rucksack, complete with a Minion poking out of it, next to us.

"I think that's been the best birthday treat I've ever had," I tell him. "I'll certainly never forget what my boyfriend did for me on my 18th."

"Really? I was afraid it'd look a bit cheap. It was only wine, chips and a few 2ps."

"No, it wasn't. It was a thoughtful idea. It was fun. I loved it." I kiss him, keen to show him how grateful I am.

Back on my doorstep, we say goodbye. I won't see him tonight because he's got to be up at five tomorrow. He's going to London for that meeting. I wish him well and I mean it, but deep down I still can't shake off the niggling fear that, once he's got this part, he'll forget about me. Why settle for a Sixth Former when he'll be meeting all sorts of celebrities – when he's a celebrity himself?

He says he loves me before he leaves. I hope so, I really hope so.

CHAPTER 17

I thought getting through my driving test was the most nerve-wracking experience of my life. Take it from me, it's nothing compared with when you drive a car on your own for the first time. No Tess with her dual controls in the seat opposite, no Jay chatting away next to me, where we're on his path with no other cars around. Now it's just me... and a road full of other cars.

Still, I made it into school alive. I was so afraid of misjudging the distance when parking and bumping one of the teachers' cars that I parked pretty much in a different postcode from the Sixth Form block, but I don't care. I'm here. I'll get more confident about driving alone with time... I hope.

Alex asked if he could come round to the

house tomorrow night for my birthday. I told him he could, but we wouldn't really be able to do anything because Mum would be home. Shame. I'd have loved to have marked my 18th birthday with a...

"Are you listening, love?" Mum asks me.

Oops, evidently not. I don't know what she's been talking about.

"You'll have to sort your own tea out tomorrow night. I'll be out."

I'm a bit surprised by this.

"What? On my birthday? My 18th as well?"

I know. I'm going to have the place to myself after all and I find this irritating. For a straight A- student, sometimes I can a bit slow on the uptake.

Mum looks at me.

"Oh come on, Zo. We haven't done anything actually on your birthday since that meal we went to when you were fourteen, and you moaned about being surrounded by couples. We're going out on Saturday night, aren't we? It's not like I'm forgetting about it or anything, is it?

"Sorry. I'm being a bit daft, aren't I?" Oh well, I

suppose if tonight's my last night of girldom, I'd better get all my childishness out of the way before I become an official adult tomorrow.

"Anyway, I was thinking I'd leave you a bottle of wine in the fridge, or as of tomorrow you can walk down to the offy and get your own, and some money so you can treat yourself to a takeaway. I thought you'd like the chance to have Alex round."

"Thanks Mum, it will be nice to have him with me. But anyway, what are you doing? You're not working." Mum always sticks her shift pattern chart on the noticeboard in the kitchen so I know when she'll be in or out.

Her lips twist into an embarrassed smile. "Actually, I've got a date."

"Bloody hell, Mum! A first date on Valentine's Day! No pressure there, then. What's his name? What's he like?"

I can't believe it. My mum's actually blushing.

"He's called Steve, he's forty- six, and well, I think he seems nice."

I'm really pleased. I'd love it if Mum could meet a decent bloke. She puts not meeting many men down to the unsociable hours of her job, so I wonder where she met this Steve?

"You've seen him, actually," she continues. "He's a delivery driver. We always have a little chat at the door when he brings my orders from Buy TV. First time he saw me, he said he'd processed a few of my orders at the depot, and he always wondered what the woman who buys all the stuff from the shopping channel looks like."

Well, he certainly knows what her daughter looks like, I think to myself. But then, I'm pretty sure Mum doesn't want to hear about that. At least this Steve was a gentleman about it. Yes, he winked at Alex, but he did look the other way while I was trying not to flash my knickers on the doorstep. Now I know why he asked about Mum when he dropped that parcel off. He's obviously fancied her for a while. Finally, Mum might actually get something useful out of her shopping channel addiction.

"Yeah, I know him," I say. "Go for it, Mum. I hope it works out."

So, this is it. As of today, I'm an adult. Still doesn't seem right to me. I think of adults as people who watch 'Gardener's World' and go to B&Q, not spend their Saturdays at Cafe Italia chatting with their mates. Oh well, better get used to it. I've joined their ranks now. I'll just have to tell Kate to slap me if she notices me getting weird urges to buy sensible shoes or Werthers Originals.

School is school. I blank out all the usual Valentine's Day crap, it doesn't matter to me this year. Seeing as how I've gone on so much about hating the day, I'll understand if Alex doesn't get me a Valentine card. He doesn't even have to do anything for my birthday; last Saturday was more than enough.

I get a couple of great pressies from Kate and Jay; Kate gives me a pair of earrings made of red Murano glass, which will go great with my Christmas necklace, then when I open Jay's gift, I'm really blown away. It's a designer bag which must have cost about £250.

When Jay's parents won all that money, we always said it wouldn't change anything. When we meet for coffee, we always take turns to pay and I've never asked him to lend me anything more than the odd tenner that any mates might borrow from each other – and I always pay him back quickly. Mind you, the only time he's ever asked to borrow from me was one time we were shopping and this small menswear shop refused to believe someone his age could have a gold card.

The bag's amazing. I'm dumbstruck.

"Do you like it? Is it too much? Look, if you think Alex will be pissed off, I can take it back..."

"Like Hell you will!" I say. If it's going back, it won't be because of anything Alex might think. "Look, Jay, I love it, but are you sure? It must have cost a bomb."

"Don't get used to it, you're getting something from Poundland next year!" he says. "I don't want to seem like a big show-off..."

"You're not, Jay. No-one thinks that," I reassure him.

He continues, "I just wanted to get you something a bit special for your 18th. For being such a good mate all these years."

The rest of the day passes by in the usual blur of schoolwork, and, at the back of my mind, nerves about driving home. This is still only my second day of driving to school, and I'm still gripping the steering wheel like I'm on a white-knuckle ride. Mum says one day, I'll start the engine, then find I've arrived at my destination without remembering anything about the journey because I've relaxed enough. That seems a million miles away at the moment.

This morning, when I arrived at school, Alex found me in the common room and wished me a happy birthday, but said I'd have to wait until the evening for my present.

When lessons are over for the day, even though he lives walking distance from school, I offer him a lift home - partly because I can, but mostly because it'll be someone else in the car with me while I'm still so nervous. When we stop at the first set of traffic lights, Alex notices my hand, gripping the gearstick as if it could slip out of my grasp. He reaches across and gives my hand a gentle pump.

"I don't know what you're worried about, babe, you're doing fine."

True enough, I haven't stalled or been beeped at, but I'm still really wary of doing something wrong.

"Why don't you try putting the radio on? It might make you feel bit calmer."

The car's got a socket I could plug my phone into, and the usual CD and radio, but I'd deliberately avoided putting any music on because I didn't want any distractions. However, when he says that, I think that, actually, maybe some background music or chatter would help. It works in lots of other situations.

"Go on, then."

He turns the radio on and finds our local station, Riverside FM. As you might imagine, they're doing a Valentine's request hour. After we've suffered a couple of sloppy ballads, the DJ moves on to the next dedication.

"This next one's for a young lady called Zoe Thompson..."

What? I allow myself to look sideways at Alex, who gives me a 'nothing to do with me,' sort of look.

"This song's from someone who loves you and says you'll know who they are... sounds like you've got a secret admirer!"

The song starts playing. Alex is irritated. Not with me, with this person who, understandably, he sees as trying to pinch his girlfriend.

"Who the hell's that, then? Who's sending you messages on the bloody radio? Everyone at school knows I'm with you." The he hears a few lines of the song and says, "Whoever they are, they've got weird taste in music. This song's well old."

I know the song. I used to like it when I was really little. It's called 'Superstar' and it's by that one who's on 'Loose Women' now, but she used to be a singer. It was a big hit when I was about four or five. It brings back memories of being picked up and swung round the living room, while this song was sung to me. I haven't heard it in a long time.

"Oh don't worry, Alex. I haven't got a secret admirer. That's my dad."

CHAPTER 18

As I drive on, there's a million questions competing for airspace in my brain, but I can't answer any of them, mostly because Alex is still fuming.

"What's he think he's doing? He buggers off for ten years and thinks he can just play you a song on the radio and it'll all be fine? I hate men like him."

I automatically open my mouth to tell him not to slag off my dad, but then I think, what has my 'dad' done to deserve any sympathy or defending from me? Not much really, so I let it go.

After I've dropped Alex off (he's going to change and come round to mine and we'll have that takeaway together later), I allow myself to think about it. Okay, I can understand him getting in contact when I'm eighteen, but why do it through the radio? We haven't moved house, so why not just send a letter? Also, why wouldn't he mention that it was my birthday? Why was it presented like a Valentine's Day message?

Either way, I decide this is not something I'm going to talk to Mum about tonight. I will tell her, just not right now. I don't want to make her angry or unhappy before she goes on her date. I'm fairly sure she won't have heard it, she doesn't tend to have the radio on in the house.

When I get in, she's got her hair in rollers and asks my opinion about which of two dresses she should wear. She actually looks excited, and if I'm honest, my mum never gets excited about anything much. If anything, possibly her favourite brand of skin cream being on half price when Buy TV have Discount Hour. I think being a single parent and having a tough job have taken the ability to get excited out of her.

I show her my earrings and the bag. She admires them both and says, "Ooh love, you've been lucky."

Yes, I have, I think. Not with the presents,

with the mates. And her. And Alex. I've got everything I need. If Dad's trying to get in touch with me again, he can shove it.

About half an hour after Mum goes out, Alex arrives. He throws off his coat and gives me a much better kiss than the polite dab on the lips I got at school this morning.

"Are you all right after before, babe? That thing with your dad hasn't upset you at all, has it?"

"Oh no, honestly. I haven't even thought about it." That's obviously not true, but I'm certainly not going to look back at this night and realise I allowed my dad to ruin it.

"Yeah, forget about him. He forgot about you for ten years. Anyway, sit down and I'll give you your pressie."

He gives me two boxes. One for my birthday and one for Valentine's, he says. Two cards as well. My first ever Valentine. You know, I could come to like this day after all.

The Valentine gift is a bottle of perfume, one he already knows I like: J'Adore.

"Thought it seemed perfect for today," he says, smiling at the sight of me spraying a little on my wrists and sniffing. "Open your birthday present now."

I take off the wrapping paper and see that whatever it is, it's from a jeweller's. Looks quite posh. Maybe panto chorus work pays better than I thought.

It's a charm bracelet. Not one of those nasty-looking yellow gold ones you see in catalogues with a load of clowns hanging off them, but a three colour gold chain, with one charm on it: a tiny, not too large or in-your-face, number 18.

"I was thinking, I could get you a new charm each year."

Oh wow. I know we talked about babies and future Christmases, but this is a solid indication of the permanence of his feelings. Bloody hell, I think, it's not far off being an engagement ring if he's genuinely thinking we've got years ahead for him to give me more charms to put on it.

"It's absolutely gorgeous, Alex. I love it, and I love you."

"I love you too, Zo. Happy birthday."

I give him the bookmark, which he loves, then we're then locked into about five minutes of passionate kissing. He begins to lean over me, as if to get me to lie on the couch so he can get on top, but I sit up.

"Actually, I think we should order some food first. It'll take ages tonight, because all the old married couples who have to stay in with their kids will be getting takeaways." I pick up the menu leaflet. "Right, what shall we order?"

I was right. Well, I know what this night is like for restaurants being busy, don't I? They tell us they can deliver our order in about ninety minutes.

"Right then," I say, putting my phone down. "Where were we?"

He walks over to me, putting his arms round me and grabbing my bum with both hands. Our bodies are touching and I can feel myself getting all tingly just thinking about what we're going to do.

"Well, I was just about to take my woman," he pauses, obviously saying the word 'woman' for effect and moving his left hand up so that he's twisting his fingers gently in my hair, "upstairs so I can make love to her."

I know he's really trying to sound romantic, but I still can't get used to being called 'woman'. I decide to play with him a little.

"There's no women round here, so will I do?"
We kiss, holding each other tightly. His
erection presses into me. Mmm, I change my
mind about wasting much more time chatting.
Trying to sound forceful and in control, I say,
"Anyway, how do you know I want that?
Maybe I'm not in the mood for all that rose
petals on the bed stuff. I might just be in the
mood for a good hard shag on the landing."

His eyes widen, and yep, there's that smile.

"Really, babe? I mean, you know I love you,
and all," he gabbles, "but I love it when you
get all horny on me. Right then missus, get up
those stairs now."

Hand on the bum again. His eyes narrow a
little as he gazes intently into mine and
whispers, "I'm going to make you scream."

We both run up the stairs and, it's not quite
an on the landing job, we do make it into my
room, but it's clear how turned on we both
are. No time for undressing each other, we
just pull our clothes off quickly and he
presses me down onto the bed. We've tried me
going on top a few times, but it's not really my
favourite. I love the feeling of his weight on top
of me. His face is just a couple of inches above
mine as he asks me what I want. I'm so
aroused already, I don't want to mess around.

"Just do me now," I say urgently. I can't wait.

Once he's inside, he takes my arms, raises them above my head and holds them down at the wrists. I love it when he does that. It makes me feel like he's taking control and I can totally let go; all I have to do is lie back and enjoy him giving me pleasure. I do it to him sometimes as well, usually when I'm teasing him by making him beg for a blow job.

He starts thrusting towards me, and I push against him so the penetration feels deeper. With each thrust, I moan; quietly at first, but getting louder as we both finish together. Once I apologised for making so much noise, yelling so close to his ear. He said he took it as a massive compliment and he loves knowing how much he's rocking my world, so now I don't hold back. Those times when we have to have sex in silence because our parents are in the next room can be a real challenge.

When we're done, and he's checked the condom (we're both still paranoid about that happening again), I lie with my head on his chest. They won't be knocking on the door with the food for another hour and I'm not finished with him yet.

While we're waiting, I bring up something that's been on my mind since I've been with him. I've never been sure when to bring it up, and even as I'm saying it, I don't know if now's the right time – or even if there ever will be a right time.

Well, too late now.

"Alex, you know Jay's party? The night we got together? You know that was... my first time."

He lets out a little laugh, before realising he should stop himself.

"Yeah, babe. You were terrified, I could see."

"It wasn't yours though, was it?"

His face alters, as he knows what I'm going to ask next.

"No, it wasn't. Babe, if you want to know how many others there were before you, that's easy. One."

Suddenly, I realise why I've avoided touching this subject for so long. Maybe because I can't believe I was able to get someone as hot as him, maybe because I didn't have much confidence before I was with him, but whatever answer he gave me, I knew I wasn't going to like it: If he'd said ten, I'd have been horrified. He's said one, so that makes me think they were in love or something.

I should just leave it there, but you know me. I can't be sensible sometimes.

"Who was she? It is someone from school? How long did you go out for?" I start pepper-spraying him with questions. The only good thing I can think is, at least I know it wasn't Sasha.

"She was a girl from my drama academy. Her name was Charlie."

Oh great. I didn't ask for the bitch's name. Now I'm going to have that stuck in my mind. The way it's obviously stuck in his.

"We were only together about six weeks, and we only did it three times," he said. "Not everyone's got a mum who works nights as often as yours."

"Three times?" I'm incredulous. "But you're so confident, you knew all the right things to do when we..."

"Zo, it wasn't hard to see it was your first time. You were practically shaking. It was just common sense to take things gently. As for everything else, well, I watch a lot of films – and appearing confident is part of what I do."

There's one last thing I want to know. I'm obviously a pretty transparent character, because he answers it for me before I say anything.

"We split up when she got bored of the drama group and stopped coming. I texted her a couple of times, asking her why she wasn't serious about acting. She just didn't reply and I took that as the end of it. I didn't chase after her. I'll be honest with you, babe, I wasn't even bothered that much. I know that sounds mean, but it was a lot easier to get over than I thought. It certainly wasn't love. The day you passed your test, remember I said I'd never told anyone I loved them before? I meant that."

"I know. I could feel your heart pounding through your shirt." I put my hand across his chest, a possessive gesture, almost as if I'm claiming him. "I'm sorry I brought that up. If you want, you can interrogate me about going to Macdonalds and bowling for two weeks with Adam Parker who does History."

"You and him?" He makes a face. "Really? Wouldn't have thought he's your type."

"He wasn't, was he?" I smile. "My type's right here, with me. I'm so glad I've got you."

"I meant what I said, Zo," he says, looking at me seriously. "I've never loved anyone before you... I don't think I could ever love anyone else."

I should say something heartfelt and meaningful to him in return, but that's just knocked me sideways. I'm overcome.

These best I can manage is, "Oh, me too," as he leans over, pressing me back onto the pillow for an intense, lingering kiss.

I've always known how much I love him; now I know I'm going to love him forever... and that he's choosing the film next time we have a night in.

CHAPTER 19

Right, so what do I do about my dad making contact with me? Alex has made his opinion pretty clear: just ignore him. Kate says call the radio station; he might have left his details with them. Jay's not sure. Neither am I. I know I said he could shove it the other day, but I can't help thinking about him.

I've always known he was out there somewhere, but I just accepted the idea that he didn't care anything about me. That message on the radio has got to me though: that song, the one he used to sing, dancing around the living room with me... he was obviously trying to get through to me with that. Mission accomplished.

I still haven't mentioned it to Mum. Her date with Steve went well and they're going to meet up again. It might be best to just say nothing.

Or, do I open the letter I received three days ago? Without even opening it, I know it'll be from him. The only other person who still sends me anything through the post is Nan, and I know it's not her handwriting. It's got to be him.

I can't do it. I can't bin it and never know what he was going to say. I rip it open and prise the sheets of surprisingly smart watermarked paper open:

Dear Zoe,

Hello, baby girl. If you're reading, this, then I guess you haven't moved house. That was why I put that message on the radio, because I wasn't sure if you'd have moved, but in the end I thought this was worth a shot.

There are so many things I want to say to you, but I want the chance to do it in person. Please call me so we can meet and discuss things. If you don't call me, then I want you be happy, and I'm sorry.

Dad,

Underneath where he's written 'Dad', there's a mobile number.

Well, there it is. There's no point speaking to my friends again, they've all made their views perfectly clear and it hasn't helped me decide. No, I need to tell Mum and see what she thinks.

I have to pick my time carefully. Of course, I go for a Tuesday night, while she's watching 'Holby City', because we all know how well that went last time I tried to discuss something important.

"Mum?" I mute the TV. "I need to tell you something important."

Her face freezes, as though she's waiting for me to tell her I'm pregnant or something. Why is that the first thing parents think of when you say you've got a problem?

"This came for me through the post. What would you do with it?"

She takes a minute or two to read it, then says, "Well, you're eighteen now. You can do what you like, love, but as far as I'm concerned, he stopped existing the day he left me to bring you up on my own."

That's that then. No hope of any happy family

reunion. If I do contact him, I'm doing it on my own.

Almost a week later, I still can't decide what, if anything, to do about my dad. I don't feel too guilty about taking time to think about it; he left me dangling for long enough. In the meantime, something else is occupying my thoughts: Alex's final call-back. The read-through with his prospective on-screen dad went well, and we thought that'd be it. Not quite. He's got to have one more meeting with the casting directors, which will decide whether or not he gets the part as a regular, established member of the 'Croft Estate' cast. The Hartleys are one of the soap's original families, been there since the show began, so if he can fit in...

...he'll move to London, Kellie Ashton will get her claws into him and I'll lose him. Why would he bother to keep in touch with me once he's made it?

Once again, I put that from my mind. I park up at school (it's true, eventually you do just drive without thinking about it) and head towards the common room. Since my school is a combined Sixth Form, I have some of my lessons in the boys' school; today is one of those days.

Passing a group of Year 10s, I hear them call, just loud enough for me to hear, "Zoe, give us a blowie."

No, I didn't hear that. I'm imagining things. I keep walking.

I'm not imagining the next group of lads who say it, though. What the fuck's going on? I look behind me, to see three lads sniggering at me.

Kate comes rushing up to me, just as I switch my phone on to see if I've got any messages.

"Zo, don't even look on Instagram. I've put up a message saying they're talking shit."

Okay. Would you not look at Instagram after being told that, even by your best friend?

There's a picture of me. The one I had taken for the Year 11 Yearbook. My hair was terrible that day because we had swimming the lesson before. Underneath is a caption: "Zoe Thompson gives free blowjobs in the library 'cause she's a sad little slag!"

What? Why would anyone do this to me?

No reason, unless they were a nasty little skank who I'd pissed off the other week, and who got turned down by my boyfriend. It's obvious who's behind this.

I look at Kate.

"I'm going to fucking kill her."

Kate tries to be reasonable, saying, "I want to do that as well, Zo, but come on. Girls like her always get away with it. You'll be the one who gets in the shit, even if she did start it. Anyway, we shouldn't come down to her level. Maybe we should just ignore her."

It's easy to say that when it's not you being advertised as offering blowjobs on the internet, I think, but I agree she's right. Anyway, what else can I do?

I can feel a few people giving me funny looks during English. I think I can hear a couple of other students whisper about it, before Miss tells them to stop talking. I decide the best course of action is to just not rise to it and ignore them. I sit next to Alex, pairing off with him when we have to discuss today's extract and say nothing.

Then, at lunchtime, it all kicks off.

The Sixth Form canteen area is shut for some repairs or something, so we have to go to the main school one, which is full of little kids. Of all the times. I'm with Kate, Jay and Alex. They've all been determined not to leave me alone while this is happening. Mr Burton is doing his thing of being seen around the school by sitting at a table with some Year Sevens. Sasha is on a table in the corner, with her gang of over made-up bitches.

Despite what I said earlier, I know I haven't really got the guts to go up to Sasha and challenge her about it. I can see her across the canteen, laughing and staring at me, but I decide she's not worth getting angry over. All I want to do is finish lunch and leave, so when another kid, maybe Year Nine, says the same thing as the lads this morning had to me as he walks past, I'd be more than happy to just let it go.

Alex isn't, though. He springs up and stands in front of the boy.

"What did you say? Say it again, go on." He's right in the kid's face.

"Alex, leave it, I'm not even bothered," I shout over, trying to stop him.

The kid isn't at all worried. I'd have died rather than front a Sixth Former when I was his age, but they don't seem to care anymore.

"I said, 'Zoe, give us a blowie'. She's a slag. It's

going round everywhere. Everyone's seen it."

The canteen has stopped and everyone's looking at them now.

For a second, I'm afraid Alex is going to punch him, but I should have known he wouldn't. Instead, he walks towards me. He stands right next to where I'm sitting, puts his hand on my shoulder and says, "It's all shit. She wouldn't... and she wouldn't blow you if you were the last person on Earth, you little nob."

Oh great, here comes Burton. That'll help.

"Alexander, sit down and leave that younger student alone. This is a serious..."

Jay stands up.

"Sir, someone's spreading rumours about Zoe online. Nasty, false rumours. And we all know who it is..." he says, looking over at Sasha.

Sasha doesn't even try to look innocent. She actually laughs.

"Oh, I see Zoe Blowie's got her panto clown and her pet faggot fighting her battles for her."

Alex steps towards Mr Burton. He's only a foot away from him.

"Sir, come on. You'll have to check Sasha's

phone or whatever to prove the Instagram
thing, but she was just out of order to Jay and
you saw that. That's homophobic. What are
you going to do?"

Mr Burton's face darkens as he tries to assert
some authority over this situation.

"Well, for a start, Alexander, you can sit down
and stop throwing accusations around."

Alex is furious. I've never seen him like this
before.

"What? You're not going to say anything to
her? Why am I getting the blame?"

Mr Burton is aware that most of the school
are watching him.

"That's it, Alexander. Go and wait outside my
office."

Alex picks up his bag and returns to his
position in front of Burton. He looks him
straight in the eye.

"Why? So you can send me home even though
all I've done is stand up for Zoe and Jay? No
problem, I'm going. And I'm not coming back.
I've had enough of this."

He walks out of the canteen, only pausing at
the door and turning to shout, right across the

room,

"And my name's Alexei, you stupid prick!"

There's a moment's silence, before the canteen erupts into a mixture of laughter and kids gossiping about what they've just witnessed. I'll give him this: he certainly found a way to stop people talking about me.

But what's going to happen to him?

I pick up my stuff and run after him. He's halfway across the yard, heading towards the gates when I catch up with him.

"Alex, what the hell are you doing?"

"I'm going, just like I said. That Burton's a useless dickhead. He does nothing about what's happening to you, Sasha just gets away with it, but I say one thing to him and he flips."

I feel really bad. This was my problem, not his. He didn't have to do anything, but now it looks like he's going to leave Sixth Form, his A-levels, everything.

"Alex, go back in there. If you can't face Burton, go and see someone like Miss Dey. She's alright. Say you're sorry, and maybe she can..."

203

"But I'm not sorry, Zo! Why should I be? How can I just stand there while Sasha's spreading that shit about you, and he does nothing about it?"

"What about your A levels though?"

We're at the gates now. He's still really angry. I can see his fist clenched round the strap of his rucksack.

"What about them? I've got my final callback for 'Croft' next week. If I get that, then Burton and his stupid A levels won't matter."

The security guard has come out of his mobile, where he sits and waits for anyone leaving or entering the school during the day. He opens the gate to let Alex out.

"Oh well, lad, you've saved me a job. I got a call on my radio to say I had to find you and escort you off the building. By that time I could see you coming across the yard anyway."

Alex growls, "Don't worry, this is the last time I'll be on these premises."

He looks at me.

"Come with me, Zo." He sees the look of alarm on my face and says, "No, I'm not saying leave Sixth Form completely. Just come with me now... please?"

I've never sagged off or run out of school before, but there's no way I can refuse, is there? He's just gone and given up everything he's been working on for the last two years, and he did it for me. There's no question. I have to go with him.

We go through the gates, ignoring the guard's complaint of "About bloody time." Then we head to the car park and find my car. I'm still worried about running out of school, but there's no way I can leave him to do this alone.

We drive to his house. By the time we get there, he's feeling a bit more cheerful, as if the realisation that he's fulfilled many a kid's fantasy has sunk in. He smiles as he replays the incident in the canteen over in his mind.

"I called him a stupid prick! He's had that coming for a long time. I wanted to say it every time he got my name wrong. Why couldn't the stupid nobhead just call me Alex?"

I'm finding this weird. My lovely, sweet Alex, being so aggressive and angry. Today's shown me a completely different side to him. I go into the kitchen. Maybe I should make him a cup of tea or something to calm him down.

Jess Molyneux

"What are you going to tell your parents?" I ask.

"The truth," he sniffs. "That some girl was spreading lies about you on the internet, and I chose to leave before I got kicked out for defending you. That's true, you could see he wanted to send me home even before I called him a prick."

Everything he says is true, but I just hope Tom and Sandra's fondness for me extends to not killing me when they find out I've pretty much caused their son to throw the last two years of his life down the toilet.

I bring our drinks in from the kitchen and we flop on the couch. It's nearly two o'clock by now. We sit for a few minutes, not sure what to do because neither of us would normally be there. To be fair, I imagine he's probably feeling a lot weirder than I am.

He finishes his tea and places the mug on the table in front of us.

"So, I'm a free man now." He snuggles into me and put his arm across my body. "No school tomorrow, nothing I have to do..."

"Erm, unless you 're a dead man tomorrow when your parents find out about this." He may be relaxed about all of this, but I'm not.

Also, what's going to happen when I go back tomorrow?

He plants a kiss on my lips and smiles. "You know what, babe? I think they'll be okay about it. They know I'm going to work in acting, one way or another. Doing Theatre Studies has been interesting, but essentially you don't need qualifications to be an actor, you just need a lucky break - and I've had one of them, haven't I?"

It's true, I think. He is sure to get the part in 'Croft Estate.' I still feel a lot more nervous about it than he does, though.

He comes in a bit closer. I rest my head on his shoulder for a moment, before turning it to kiss him. He starts stroking my boobs until he's touching my nipples through the fabric of my blouse. My hands wander down to his groin to return the favour, but I don't need to do anything. He's already got a solid erection under his jeans.

I have to laugh. "Alex, is there any situation that doesn't give you a massive hard-on? What are you like at funerals?"

"Depends if they were fit or not," he laughs. "Anyway, I don't have to pick Leo up from football until half four. Are we shagging or what?"

I know today's been a bit crazy, but there's something very powerful about the thought that he was willing to take such a big risk to defend my reputation. I'd even give that reverse cowgirl a go for him right now. In fact, right now I think I'd probably even swallow if he wanted me to, but I'm not volunteering that information; I'll wait and see if he asks.

CHAPTER 20

Oh my God.

I don't know if he was on a bit of a high from walking out of school at lunchtime, or whatever, but when we went up to his bedroom, it was incredible. He was incredible. He needs to tell Burton he's a stupid prick more often if this is what happens.

As soon as we got into his room, we took our clothes off quickly, but instead him lying me on the bed, he pinned me against the wall as he said, "I've always wanted to try this. I'm going to take you up against the wall."

He's several inches taller than me, so he had to bend to begin with, but once he was in, he lifted me up so my feet were off the floor. It was a bit uncomfortable, having my back against the hard wall rather than a nice, soft mattress, but the feeling of him grinding into me more than compensated. He held me up by putting his hands under my bum while I locked my legs around him.

We couldn't hold that position for long, so we moved across to the bed, where he was able to satisfy me by thrusting in deeper, making me scream with delight. He leaned up on his elbows, doing all the work with his pelvis. With me pushing against him for maximum effect, it didn't take long until we were both exhausted; we then curled up in each others' arms, smiling and a little sleepy.

That was definitely better than General Studies.

Eventually, after we've been lazily chatting and holding each other for about half an hour, his tone becomes a bit more serious.

"Babe. I want to say thanks for this afternoon. For you standing by me, I mean."

"Alex," I look up at him from where I've got my head on his chest. "How could I do anything else? I love you. I'd do anything for you."

"Will you stay here 'til my parents get back and I explain what happened? I just want you with me when I talk to them."

Oh bollocks. I have to admit, I don't fancy that much. I still reckon they'll blame me for it. I can't refuse after what I've just said though, can I?

"'Course I will," I tell him. "I'm sure they'll understand."

We drive round to Leo's school to fetch him, then Alex gets rid of him upstairs with the bribe of watching the telly in his room.

Sandra arrives home first. Alex and I are sitting on the couch, drinking tea. As soon as she comes in, Alex pours one for her. Sandra takes it and sits down on the armchair opposite us, saying nothing. I guess she's had a phone call from Burton this afternoon, then.

"I don't want to seem rude, Zoe, but I'd like to speak to Alexei alone, so I think perhaps you should go home now."

Oh dear, he's getting the full name. The only other time I've seen her do that is his birthday, when she was referring to his Russian roots. Otherwise, she calls him Alex. This can't be good. Also, if she wants me to go, it sounds like she's going to start slagging me off the minute I'm out the door.

It's her house. I can't exactly refuse to leave, but I promised Alex I'd stay. I look nervously at him, to see what he wants me to do.

"Mum, I want Zo to stay. She didn't tell me to do what I did today, this isn't her fault."

Sandra takes a sip of her tea. She's not happy, I can see that. I guess it's bad enough her son's throwing his A Levels out of the window in the Spring of Year 13, but now he's going against his mother, in favour of his girlfriend. Oh God, she's going to hate me.

"Fine, she can stay I suppose. What on earth were you thinking when you said that to your headteacher?"

"Oh come on Mum, it's only what you called Dad that time he recorded over your wedding video..."

Sandra glares at him. This was not the time for a flippant answer. Alex realises how angry she is and tries again.

"It wasn't fair, Mum. There was this girl spreading rumours about Zo online, so we told Burton and he didn't even say anything to her. Then the same girl skitted Jay, Zo's mate, because he's gay."

A wave of surprise crosses Sandra's face. I guess Burton was selective about which parts of what happened at lunchtime he told her.

"He still didn't do anything, then I just lost it when he got my name wrong again. I know it doesn't sound like a big deal, but any time he's spoken to me, he's called me Alexander ever since I started that Sixth Form and it just pisses me off."

Sandra listens to everything he has to say, lips pursed. I wish she'd say something. Eventually, she puts her mug on the coffee table and says, "Well, there's still no excuse for calling the head a ... well, what you said, but I can understand your reasons."

Alex can sense she's not going to kill him after all.

"I'm not going back there, Mum, so don't even suggest I go back and grovel."

She gets up and takes her mug back to the kitchen.

"I'm not going to say that, love... as long as you get this part in the soap. If you get that, fine. If you don't, well you're going to have to go back in September, if they'll have you. And all this is dependent on your father agreeing to it as well."

Alex looks more relaxed, and I feel better. He follows her out to the kitchen. I stay in the living room and check my phone. There's texts from Jay and Kate, asking where I am and if Alex is okay. While I write replies, I can hear Sandra and Alex talking as he rinses out the mugs.

"Thanks, Mum. I wasn't sure you'd understand, but..."

"Alex, I've known everything about you since before you were born. One of the things I love about you is that you can't stand by when you see injustice. True, you shouldn't have lost your temper, but I'm not surprised you wouldn't allow someone to hurt Zoe, or this James boy."

Alex laughs. "He's Jason, actually. Got to get it right, had enough problems with names today. I don't regret what I did, Mum. I couldn't let those kids go round saying those things about her."

"You really love her, don't you?"

"Yeah, I do. But Mum, I really want this part in 'Croft', well, I need it now, but I'm worried about being apart from her if I get it."

"Oh love," I hear her say, from where I'm motionless on the couch, listening intently, "if it's meant to be, nothing will keep you apart."

CHAPTER 21

Alex and his dad drive down to London at the weekend for the final callback. He calls me afterwards and says he feels it went well. While I've got a weekend without him, I think I'd better concentrate on my coursework and make a decision about my other recent problem, which I've been pushing to the back of my mind: Dad.

In the end, I don't think I can phone him. I'd go to bits and not know what to say. I decide to get in touch with a text, suggesting I meet him somewhere. Coming round to our house – the house he used to live in with Mum – is out of the question. No, I'll pick the venue and the time. He's going to do this my way, on my territory.

He returns my text after about half an hour,

agreeing to meet me at Café Italia tomorrow.

Getting ready to go on a date is tough. Getting ready to meet the father you haven't seen in ten years is a whole other level of tough. What do I wear? Usually, getting ready for a date, I'd be aiming to make myself look as sexy as possible – hardly what I should be going for now. For a minute I think maybe I should just show up in scruffy clothes, as a way of showing him I don't care too much what he thinks – and surely it should be me he wants to see, not what I'm wearing?

It's not true that I don't care, though. I've been lying awake for a few nights, trying to imagine how this meeting's going to go. I'm not even sure what to say at the beginning: I'm certainly not running up to him and throwing my arms around him like in a film, but I don't want to storm in and start laying into him about the last ten years either. That'd probably just make him turn and leave.

In the end, I reckon I'll just start with, "Hello" and see where it goes from there.

I get to the café about half an hour before our arranged time. I want to make absolutely sure I'm the one there first, to see him when he walks in. I hope I'll still recognise him. He'll be ten years older, so I'm trying to picture a slightly more grey and wrinkled version of my memories, but hopefully he won't have gained or lost loads of weight or anything else that'd make him hard to spot. I wonder if he still wears the same sort of clothes?

At two o'clock, he arrives. He's forty-seven now, so sure enough, his hair is flecked with grey rather than the black I remember. He's wearing a suit, but it doesn't look particularly expensive. Damn, he hasn't tracked me down to tell me he's won the lottery then, I think to myself. At least he looks reasonably healthy. Another thing I'd been worried about was that he could be contacting me because he was ill.

He looks around the café, uncertainly. I guess he hasn't been here before. This place has only been open for two years; I assume he's been out of the area completely.

When his eyes finally find the corner table where I'm sitting, his whole body visibly freezes. Then, after a few seconds, he starts walking towards me as if he's afraid of me. When he stops at my table, I raise my eyes towards him, but I don't get up.

"Zoe, it's you," he says, opening his arms to hug me. I allow it to happen. I've hugged lots of people and meant nothing by it. It's just a greeting.

"Hello," I reply.

Not 'Hello, Dad.' I'm not willing to give him that yet, not until I've heard what he's got to say.

Before he sits down, he offers to get me a coffee. I've finished the one I had, so I accept a caramel latte from him. When he comes back from the counter, he sits with his forearms on the table, leaning in towards me.

"You must have a lot of questions." I guess that's his invitation for me to ask them.

Strangely enough, I don't have a lot. Just one.

"Why have you left this so long, Dad?"

There. I called him Dad. Already. So much for me acting cool and making him stress out a bit. I'll be sitting on his knee by the end of the afternoon. I'm such a pushover sometimes.

He sighs. "Zoe, I knew you'd ask this, so you think I'd have prepared a decent answer, wouldn't you? The truth is, I don't really know. I suppose I wanted to wait until you were eighteen and Gemma couldn't stop me getting in touch."

"Yeah, well she knows I'm here now, but she just said I can do it if I want. She isn't stopping me, but she's not very enthusiastic about it."

He raises his eyebrows as he takes a sip of his drink. "Enthusiasm and your mother never did go hand in hand."

This sounds like the conversation I had with Mum that time. Even though that ended pretty badly, I have to know. After all, I've got no idea if it might be ten years 'til I see him again.

"Dad, did you leave because you didn't love Mum? Or, I mean, had you stopped loving her, but you did love her at first? Or did you never really love her?"

He doesn't reply immediately. Admittedly, I phrased that so badly I suppose it'd be fair enough if he asked me to explain what the hell I meant.

"Depends what you mean by love. Did I think I could spend the rest of my life with her? No. Did I want to hurt her? Also, no. I just thought it might be the best thing for us both to start again. You were in school, settled. So I had to go."

Okay, I think, I can accept that... even if he hasn't really answered the question. There's still one thing I have to ask, though. Again, despite my efforts to appear calm and unconcerned, as if I can take or leave him, my voice gives me away. So do my eyes, which are getting all glassy. I don't want to cry in front of him, but I don't know if I'm going to be able to stop myself.

"Alright, couples split up. Fine. Why did you just disappear though? How 'settled' do you think I felt for months after you left, wondering when, or even if, you'd come back? I was eight years old. I had no idea what had happened to you."

He reaches out to touch my arm, but I sit back on my chair so he can't. It's a bit late to be my caring dad now. He reaches into his jacket pocket, finds a clean cotton handkerchief and places that in front of me. I take it, but not without huffing angrily as if he's just spat on the table.

Once I've dried my eyes, I look at him, waiting for an answer.

"There is no real explanation, Zoe. I'm sorry. I was thirty-seven, I wasn't even a daft kid. Things were going badly with your mother, work was terrible, and I just snapped one day and escaped them both."

"And me. Don't forget about escaping from the hassle of having to be around me."

His face falls. He know he deserves any anger I aim at him, and he's going to have to take it.

"Believe me, Zoe, that is the biggest regret of my life. If I could go back and change that..."

"You can't though, can you?" I interrupt. "I've had ten years without a dad, and that's gone forever." I take a deep breath. "Still, I can fill you in if you want the condensed catch-up version. I've got ten GCSEs, I'm still mates with little Jason from down the road, except he's not little or from down the road any more, I've been mates with a girl called Kate since Year 7, I'm hoping to get into Manchester if my A levels are good enough, I passed my driving test a few months ago and I've got a boyfriend called Alex."

He smiles, and this time he's the one looking a bit teary-eyed.

"That's fantastic, love. I wondered if you'd have passed some exams when you were sixteen. I thought about ringing some schools in this area to ask, but I thought they probably wouldn't tell me." Then he asks, "Alex. What's he like, then? I hope he's..."

My voice rises. "He's what? Good enough for me? He's a lot better than someone who just leaves and then waltzes back into my life after ten years, so he's better than you already."

He looks really hurt now, and I think that may have been a bit harsh. He is still the man who used to pick me up and swing me round the living room to that song, who used to take me to the canal and try to get me interested in fishing in the school holidays...

Oh no. I don't want to see my dad cry. Especially when it's me who's made him cry. Luckily, he manages to stop at his eyes just getting a bit moist before he recovers himself.

"I just thought you were better off without me. Both of you. That's why I stayed away. Then I thought your mum would meet someone else and you'd start calling him Dad, and you'd forget I ever existed. That's why the radio message was disguised as a Valentine. I wasn't sure if you still thought of me as your dad anymore."

This time, I reach out and touch his hand. "That never happened. I'll admit Mum and I don't mention you much, and we've got on fine without you, but no other man has ever been my dad." I pause. "Although that's not to say you are right now. I need more time to get my head round everything you've said today."

He holds my hand across the table, and says he'll wait as long as it takes if we can patch things up, even a little.

That seems to make things a bit better. I wouldn't say we were hugging and promising never to be apart again by the end of the afternoon, but we were at least able to have a conversation, without me sniping at him about his absence.

He never married anyone else, but I learn I've had a half-sister, Hope, for the last seven years. Unfortunately it didn't work out with her mother, either. He does say he's learned from experience and tries to see more of her than he's seen of me. She lives in Croydon. He gives me a photo of her to keep, as well as a more recent one of him. I didn't think to bring pictures, so I let him take one of me on his phone.

He's lived and worked away; Birmingham, Manchester, Bristol – anywhere except near either of his daughters, I can't stop myself thinking. He's come back for a few months he says, so he asks if we could meet again in the future.

I wouldn't say he's completely won me round, but I don't feel the anger I did before.

"I suppose so."

As we leave, we have a hug which involves both of us this time, and he kisses my cheek. I will meet him again, there's still a lot more I

want to find out. Maybe I could even bring
Alex with me next time.

 Actually, maybe not, I think. He didn't think
contacting Dad was a good idea at all, and
once you've called your headteacher a stupid
prick for getting your name wrong, who knows
what he'd say to the man who deserted me for
a decade.

CHAPTER 22

It's not the same at school without Alex. We didn't live in each other's pockets all day, but we'd have lunch together sometimes, and it was just nice to know he was around if I wanted to see him.

The day after I ran out of school to be with him, Mr Burton found me in the common room. He said he wasn't condoning what I did in any way, but he wasn't going to take any further action. All I could think was, no *further* action? You haven't taken ANY action! Sasha spreads lies about me on the internet, then says that horrible thing to Jay, and she's still here, acting like she owns the school – and Alex isn't here. How does that work, eh Sir?

As far as I'm concerned, he knew he was

wrong; he was lucky Alex or Jay's parents
didn't ring and complain, but he knew my
mum would have done... not that she knows I
skipped school. Do you think I'd tell her that?

Still, I could see there was no point
complaining. I was angry for Jay, but he said
he's always known he'd have to get tough
about that sort of thing when he came out,
and once my initial anger had died down, I
didn't care what Sasha spread around about
me. If she wanted to hurt me, I guess she got
what she wanted because now I'm alone in my
English lessons, where I used to have Alex
beside me.

I find myself texting him at every break in the
day. Now he's not going to school, his parents
have got him doing all sorts of things:
shopping, housework and working in the
stock room of his dad's shop. He's okay, and
says he doesn't regret leaving school at all, but
I can tell even he's a bit worried about when
he'll hear from the casting directors. It was
always a big deal, but it's become a lot more
important than it was before.

Anyway, today we finished school for Easter.
We're finishing a day earlier than most of the
schools in the area because of an INSET day,
so tomorrow I'm planning on surprising Alex.
His parents will be at work, Leo's primary

school won't have finished yet, and he'll be at home, alone.

But I'm not planning just going round for the usual shag in the bedroom: we still haven't done it in my car.

The plan is that we can drive to somewhere nice and quiet, where no-one can see us, and it'll be brilliant. We're going to love it.

Okay. Sex in a car is officially shit.

I came round to his house at around 11am. He'd had a shower but wasn't dressed; probably thinking it'd be the usual thing of going straight upstairs. When I sprung my idea of going for a drive on him, he was well up for it. He got his clothes on and we were ready to go.

There's an area of green land about twenty minutes' drive from where we live, so we headed straight there. Of course, we'd been talking and thinking about what we were going to do all through the journey, so we were both pretty excited. The sun was out, it was getting warm after a long Winter; it was a lovely Spring day. It should have been fantastic.

Seriously though, who ever thought that sex in a car was a good idea? I know if your mum's job doesn't cause you to have the place to yourself as often as mine's does, it might be a necessity – but I think I've been spoiled by the ready availability of a bedroom... and space.

For a start, there's the privacy. As in, there isn't any. I know my car might feel like my own personal room when I'm driving, singing along to the radio, but that doesn't quite apply to shagging! And it's illegal, which I didn't find out until afterwards. And no, there's none of that thrill that you might get caught that people always talk about. There's just the worry that you WILL get caught, filmed and end up watching yourself on a repeat of 'Rude Tube' in about six months' time. Or with your face pixelated, but not enough to stop everyone knowing it's you, on one of those police programmes.

Still, we weren't thinking about any of that at the time. We still thought we were in for a great experience at this point. I pulled over into a layby next to a field.

Once we'd unclicked our belts, he leaned over and we kissed. Not sure why, we both knew what we were there to do, but I guess it's the generally agreed starting point. The kissing was fine. It was after that when things started to get tricky.

He was in the passenger seat, so I reckoned it might be best if I moved over and sat across him. Easier said than done. My skirt (I thought that might be a good idea, I could cover up what we were doing like a sort of tent; I mightn't have known it was illegal, but I still didn't want to display everything to Farmer Giles if he was taking his cows for a walk) got caught in the gearstick, then I was surprised by how little room there was. I was having to bend my head down to avoid hitting it on the ceiling, and then he couldn't really move. He'd reclined the seat back as far as he could, but he was still in a position where it was impossible for him to insert himself into me.

We tried to shift around. Again, you wouldn't believe how awkward that was; I think my knee set off the horn, which is about as good as things got, because we fell into a genuine cuddle as we laughed about it. With me underneath him, it was no better; he was unable to bend enough to get himself in.

In the end, we gave up.

Sitting on the back seat, we held each other, realising that this was the only good bit about any of our car-based activities.

He said, "Look babe, I know I said I wanted to do this, but we tried it and it wasn't as good as I thought it'd be, was it? I'm sorry."

I didn't say anything. I just gave him a smile, which ended up breaking into a giggle.

"Oh, don't apologise, Alex. We'll look back on this and laugh. Sod it, shall we go back to yours and just be boring and traditional in a warm comfy bed?"

We both got out of the car, resumed our regular seating positions and I started the engine. I guess it's true, for some things at least: there's no place like home.

We arrive back at his house by about 1.45pm. Still loads of time before he has to collect Leo, so maybe we can make up for our rubbish car experience. We haven't had any lunch, so he makes us sandwiches and coffee. While we're eating, his phone rings. It's his agent; he's had one for the last couple of months. It's the same one Kellie Ashton's signed up with.

Again, I think she put a word in for him.

I guess this is it. He's going to find out that he's got the part, and it won't matter about him packing in school two weeks ago. They'll want him to start rehearsing and filming pretty much straight away, so he'd have had to give his A Levels up anyway.

"Hi? Yes, it is. Right."

I sit in silence, waiting for him to finish the conversation, then do something like punch the air or come and give me a delighted kiss … but his face doesn't seem to be that of someone who's been given the job of a lifetime.

"Oh, why? Will they? Sure, I'll wait to hear from you. Thanks."

What on earth's going on? Does this mean he hasn't got it? How could they not want him?

He ends the call and drops his phone down next to him on the couch.

"They're going to keep looking for someone else. Apparently they've decided they do want to try to find someone blond with blue eyes, like the original Jake was. They've had too many complaints on the 'Croft Estate' fansite about it getting totally unrealistic. They said they want someone younger as well, Jake would only be about fourteen. They've said they'll keep me in mind for other roles, but they probably always say that."

I can't believe it. All those trips to London, all that time spent preparing and practising, and then they decide they don't want him at the last minute because he's got brown hair and eyes and he's eighteen, something they knew all along? It's not fair.

He flops back onto the couch. He looks crushed.

"Oh God, Zo. You know what this means. I'm going to have to go back to school and kiss Burton's arse. Mum and Dad were only okay with me leaving as long as I got this part, and I haven't..."

His phone goes again. The display says, 'Auntie Jean'.

"Have you even got an Auntie Jean?" I ask him.

He picks the phone up and switches it to voicemail. "No, I haven't. That's Kell. She asked me to disguise her number when she gave it to me. I'll get back to her later, I'm not up to talking right now."

I feel a bit sick. Not only is he on shortened-name terms with Kellie Ashton, who did win Sexiest Female at the Soap Awards by the way, but he's got her number! Still, I know now is not the time to bring that up and anyway, he's put her onto voicemail.

Hey, that's not bad actually, is it? My boyfriend's turning down Kellie Ashton to be with me!

I put my arms round him and kiss him.

"Babe, I'm not really up for it," he says, stiffening in my arms.

"Alex, I know. I just want to make you feel better, that's all."

We stay like that, curled up in each other on the couch, while he goes over everything he thinks he did wrong, anything that could have cost him the part.

I'm not at all happy, but I can't help thinking that at least this means I won't be losing him.

CHAPTER 23

Alex is like a lost soul for a while. It's not
about not being chosen for the part; they were
very positive about him, and he's always
understood that actors don't get every part
they go for. It's the idea that this more or less
means he'll have to go back to school in
September. I could be away in Manchester,
he'll be a year older than everyone else and,
worst of all, he'll have to go grovelling to
Burton.

I do my best to cheer him up. I do things like
take him to the cinema and we repeat the
chocolate-baton-and-wine picnic on the
beach. The weather's nicer by April, but I
actually liked it better when we did it for my
birthday because there was no-one else
around. It's not the same trying to have a
sneaky kiss, then some kid's beach ball

bounces in and spoils the moment.

It's a Wednesday evening. He's come round to see me. Mum's in, so we're sitting up in my bedroom. When I tell him about how I'd met up with Dad the last time he went to London, he's surprised.

"Why would you do that, Zo? I know it's up to you and everything, but you've always said you were fine without him. "

I tell him about the main points of our conversation and how we left things: hardly all sorted out, but a lot less frosty than we were at the start. I show him the picture of Hope.

"Wow, so he messed up not once but twice," he says with disdain. "What a guy."

I find myself defending my father.

"Oh, that's a bit unfair, Alex. He does try to see Hope, mostly because he regrets not keeping in touch with me," I tell him. "And he said he stayed out my life because he thought I'd be better off without him around."

"The only thing I think I can agree with him on so far," Alex snorts. "So what are you going to do? If you see him again, do you want me to come with you?"

I have been thinking about calling him to

arrange another meeting. I'm not sure if it'd be a good idea to take Alex along if he's going to be so negative about him, but if Dad and I are going to get to know each other again, I guess at some point he's got to meet the most important man in my life.

"I guess so, but don't give him a hard time. If anyone should do that, it's me and Mum, and if I can start looking for ways to get over it, you've got to just go with me on this."

"Alright, babe. Just don't expect me to like him."

Hmm. Am I imagining it, or has Alex has gone a bit cocky since he left school? Maybe he's just being defensive; having problems trying to get his head round the fact that things aren't going the way he wanted them to right now, and unless a miracle occurs, when September comes he's going to be back at school, a year behind.

"Don't expect him to like you, either," I tease. "You've dropped out of school, you wear eyeliner and you're banging his daughter."

He looks wounded, and, just like when I was with Dad, I realise I might have gone a bit too far. I sit next to him. He looks sideways at me.

"I don't wear eyeliner all the time. And I didn't

drop out, I left on principle."

"Sorry, that was mean. But, even if he'd been around all my life, no dad likes their daughter's boyfriend, and no boyfriend likes their girl's dad. It's like some kind of law or something. I could bring Prince Harry home and he wouldn't like the look of him."

Alex's face softens a little.

"Okay, babe. I just don't see why you want to even speak to him after he walked out on you, but if you want to get to know him again, well, I'll do whatever you want."

I snuggle in a bit closer to him. "Hmm, I like sound of that... whatever I want?"

This is a bit of a risky move, jumping from a serious conversation to trying to get him interested in a shag. If I'm honest with you, we haven't really done it much recently. Since he didn't get the part, he's stayed away from me some nights, and when he has come round, sometimes we'd start kissing and touching each other, only for him to back off, saying he feels tired or something.

I'm starting to worry about it. Okay, I don't want him to be depressed, but the only other reason for him suddenly not wanting to have sex is he's gone off me. Luckily, he seems to be in a bit more of a good mood tonight. He realises what I mean, and he drops his eyebrows, fixing me with his gaze.

"Oh yeah. Anything." I move onto the bed, so I can lie down. He lies down on the bed too, and we move onto our sides so that we're facing each other.

Even though we're both still fully clothed, we lock into each other. His erection feels even bigger through his jeans, and when I lie him flat and get on top, it feels a lot less awkward than whenever we've tried it before because I'm not feeling self-conscious about him seeing my body.

I undo his jeans (I'm going to have to tell him not to wear a belt, so I can get easier access), pull them and his undies down his legs a bit, but then I have to take my jeans and knickers off, there's no way around that.

Other than that, we're both fully clothed as I position myself on top of him. I've never really liked going on top before , but when I'm not having to worry about what I look like, I have to admit it does feel good, and I can move around more. I bend down to kiss him at times, but it's best when I'm upright, because I can feel him standing upright inside me.

He starts pushing his hips forward, with his

hands clasping my hips. The rhythm of his determined, powerful thrusts, combined with my hip movements brings us both to a climax within a minute of each other. We have to try to be quiet: I'm pretty sure Mum knows what we're up to, but I don't think she really wants to hear it. Even so, I'm the happiest I've been in weeks and even he seems a bit more cheerful as well.

Oh, thank God. He's coming back to me. He's been so down for ages; it's been good to do something that makes me feel I've got my gorgeous, confident, lovely Alex back.

"I loved that," I purr as we lie together on top of the covers afterwards.

"Mmm, me too," he says. "Got to admit, I'm not sure about the clothes though. I like to be able to look at your body when you go on top. We don't do it that way often enough as it is."

A few days later, I'm at school and it's break time. Looking at my phone, I see I've got three texts from Alex. He knows the times when I'm in lessons, so this must be pretty urgent. Hope he's alright.

I'm just about to open the first one, when my phone starts ringing with an incoming call.

"Zo! It's me!" He sounds really excited. I can't even get a 'Hello' in before he continues, "Carl called me this morning, wait 'til I tell you this!"

Carl's his agent. Sounds like he's found him something else. Not that Carl actually found the 'Croft Estate' part, that was down to Kellie Ashton really. Still, it's not going to be a role in one of the country's top soap's established families, but hopefully whatever it is, it'll be something big enough that he doesn't have to go crawling back to school in the Autumn.

"'Croft Estate' called. They want me!"

I'm confused now.

"What happened? Weren't they going to go with a blond kid for Jake in the end? Can't they find one?"

"It's not the part of Jake. They're bringing in a new family, and they've seen enough of me to offer the part of the son to me straight away! Carl said they've got some really big storylines planned for me. I can't believe it, Zo."

"Oh Alex, that's fantastic news." I can't help feeling a bit wary on his behalf, though. We thought he had the part of Jake in the bag, but it all went wrong. However, it seems that he, or at least Carl, is a step ahead of me.

"Carl's getting them to fax over the contract so I can sign it this afternoon. He doesn't want to let this slip away either, obviously it's money for him as well, isn't it? Talking of money, you wouldn't believe what they've offered me! Then, I'll do some rehearsals with the actors who are playing my parents, and then I'll start filming after that. Oh Zo, I wish you were here so I could kiss you."

"Me too. Anyway, I've got to go now, Alex. I'm so happy for you. Talk to you later, bye."

"See you later, Zo. XY, Z. And, Zo? Remember, don't tell anyone yet, please? But if you can, tell Burton he's still a prick from me."

So, that's it. He's got a part in a national soap. Once the viewers see him, they'll fall in love with him as easily as I did. He's going to be famous, rich and beating the fans off with a stick. And let's not forget the biggest thing - miles away from me.

He needn't worry. I won't tell anyone. I think if I tried to speak right now, my face would collapse. The bell rings for the end of break, but instead of heading to English, I dash to the toilets where, once I've shut myself into a cubicle, I give in to heavy, wrenching sobs.

This is going to be the end for us, isn't it?

I cry for about ten minutes, sitting on a toilet with the lid down. I've got to be pleased for him. This is what he wants, the only thing he could ever do. He was born to be an actor – the fact he's been snapped up for a role like this at the age of eighteen proves it.

I try to reassure myself by remembering the conversation he had with his mum, the one I overheard. He said he really loved me, and that he was worried about leaving me. I've got to trust him. He will have fans throwing themselves at him, but he loves me. I've got to remember that.

But what good's that going to be when he's so far away? It's not like a TV series, where he'd film six episodes and then stop: soaps are on continuously. If he's going to be the important character they're planning he'll be, he'll have to move away permanently.

I know I won't want to even look at anyone else while he's away, but would we be able to make a long-distance relationship work? I guess the answer to that lies with him.

When I meet Kate at lunchtime, she can see something's wrong. I tell her about Alex's job offer. I know he asked me not to tell anyone, but I think he'd know I'd tell Kate. Telling just your best girlfriend doesn't count. Besides, I can trust her not to say anything.

"I'm not going to lie to you, Zo, it's a tough one," she says. "Whenever I see you together, it's obvious he's crazy about you, and I know you love him. It should work, but..."

"So many long-distance relationships don't, and that's before you factor in that he'll be surrounded by soap babes and going to award ceremonies all the time?"

She doesn't say anything, but I can see she's thinking, 'Well, yeah.'

"You've got to talk to him, Zo. He's the only who can really tell you if this is going to work or not."

I know she's right, but what if he says he thinks it'll be too hard to stay in touch and that we should break things off now, so he has a clean break when he leaves? I'm not sure I could handle that. I've got my A levels coming up soon. The most important exams of my life. This is not what I need.

For a second, I think about seeing if it's too late to change my UCAS application. I've applied to Manchester as a first choice, but maybe I could change to somewhere in London? I didn't want to go to London before because it's more expensive to live and people always say it's unfriendly, but I wouldn't care about anyone else if I could be with him. Maybe we could even get a flat together.

I've got to get real. It's way past the final deadline. If I want to change courses, I'd have to take a year out anyway. And then there's Mum. She'd totally flip if she found out I was changing everything I'd planned because of Alex. She likes him, but the thought of me letting a man decide the direction my life takes would kill her. She'd feel like I hadn't listened to anything she's said for the last ten years.

No. There's only one thing to do, and that's tell him how I feel. He might say it's better that we finish before he goes, despite him saying he loves me – but I'm not going to be able to stand not knowing where I am.

"I will, Kate, I will. It's going to be fine, I know it is," I say, probably with no conviction at all in my voice. "Hey, why don't we go into town after school tonight and start looking for dresses for the Sixth Form prom?"

"Are you still going, then? When Alex left I just assumed you wouldn't be interested any more."

I lean back in mock disgust.

"What, just 'cause I don't have a date, I should stay at home? No way! I'm going, I can dance with you and Jay, then maybe I'll treat Alex to a view of my dress before he helps me out of it afterwards."

As I'm speaking, the realisation of the time frame he's working to enters my head.

"Well, that is if he's still around. Anyway, we'll think about that later. Tonight we shop!"

After a fun couple of hours of trying on a few dresses, blagging as many makeup samples as we can by promising the staff on every makeup counter we'd come back to them for our prom makeup and not actually buying anything, I'm feeling a lot better. I text Mum and tell her I'm going round to see Alex.

When I get there, it's clear that there's been a bit of celebrating going on in the Ryan household. Sandra immediately offers me a drink, insisting I leave my car outside their house and come back for it in the morning. Tom and Alex are in the kitchen, drinking from cans. I've never seen Alex drink beer before. I wonder if he's doing it because he's with his dad, or does he hate the wine he drinks when I open a bottle at my house, and just doesn't feel he can say anything?

When I enter the kitchen, he walks straight towards me and gives me a tight, enthusiastic hug.

"Babe," he says, clearly a little bit drunk. "I'm so glad I've got you with me to share this."

Just hope you always feel that way, I think to myself.

Alex's phone starts buzzing on the kitchen counter. It's one of his mates, so while he fills him in on the day's developments, I talk to Tom and Sandra, learning a bit more about the character he'll be playing. It's someone by the name of Dylan Taylor and the writers are hoping he's going to become the soap's resident bad boy and pinup. Apparently he's going to get to torch a car in his first week alone.

I ask where Alex will be living. Apparently, because he's eighteen, he doesn't have to be chaperoned, but they do organise accommodation for the younger actors, especially if it's their first time living away from home. The channel usually rents a house and puts a few of the younger cast in together, sharing.

A horrible mental image of Kellie Ashton wandering around the house in her bikini enters my head, but I don't have to worry about her anymore. It's been all over the gossip mags recently about how she's just moved into a new house with someone who plays for Manchester United.

Anyway, I tell myself, it doesn't matter who they put in there; he loves you, remember? He could have had Sasha ages ago, but he didn't. It's you he wants to be with.

Alex returns to the living room. After a few minutes, he looks at me and mouths, "Do you want to go up for a bit?"

I give him a not-too-obvious nod. I'm not feeling hugely in the mood, and I'm not that sure he'd be capable of anything right now, but it would be good to have a chance to talk to him alone.

When we get up there, he hugs me again.

"Babe, this is the best day ever. I was starting to get worried about what I'd do in September if nothing came up. There was no way I was ever going back and apologising, but I know Mum and Dad wouldn't have let me sit round the house doing nothing. And this is what I've always wanted to do! I'm a proper actor. I'm in the union, I've got an agent and a proper acting job."

He kicks his trainers off and lies on the bed.

"C'mere, babe."

I look at him. "Are you sure you're up to it?"

He grins. "I'm not that drunk, I'm just happy...
I've managed it loads of other times when
we've been drinking. Come on, I really want
to." He sits up and whispers to me, "You know
what, babe? The only other thing I've been
able to think about all day is you."

"Okay," I say to him. "If you want me, tell me
what you've been thinking of doing to me all
day."

From the way he gasps, I can see it's true.
He's definitely got a few ideas. That makes me
feel so good, so desired, so ready for him...
and if he could still think of me on the day he
gets told he's got this job, it makes me feel
pretty special as well.

"Well, first," as he slides off my cardi and pulls
my T-shirt over my head, "I'd want a good,
hard look at you. Last time, when we had our
clothes on, it wasn't the same.

I'm sitting on the edge of his bed, with just my
bra and trousers on. He edges the straps
down and pushes his tongue under the lace,
teasing each nipple gently with a light nibbling
motion. I give what I've learned to call a 'silent
moan': when you can't make any noise

because of parents or little brothers in the next room, but you've got to let him know how amazing he is.

He's clearly enjoying himself. He reaches round my back, undoes the bra and throws it to the floor, before lying on top of me and continuing with his teasing. After a few minutes, when I think I can't be silent any longer, he raises his face towards mine and stares hard at me.

"Oh, Zo. Your tits are gorgeous. I could do that all night. I just want to do everything that makes you happy."

No you can't, I'm thinking to myself. I want the feeling of you inside me now. I'm not sure I can wait any longer... funny how you can suddenly feel up for it after a bit of nip attention.

However, I decide to take him at his word. I slip my trousers and knickers off, lie on the bed and take his hand... then I move it downwards.

"Touch me."

His eyes widen at the thought. I can see he's a bit surprised. I've never been up for masturbation before, and I've certainly never asked him to do this.

Why the hell have I waited so long? His quick fingers stroke up and down, making me writhe in almost painful ecstasy. Then he slips two fingers inside me, moving them back and forth until I have to beg him to stop because I'm worried I'll scream the house down.

"You enjoy that, then?" he asks, totally unnecessarily.

I'm unable to answer him. I'm lying next to him, out of breath. He lies next to me, on his side.

"What do you want me to do next, babe?"

I say nothing, but start to undo the button on his jeans, without once losing eye contact with him. He knows exactly what I want.

He positions himself on top of me, then I use my hand to guide him inside. Oh, man. His fingers are fine, but they can never replace the real thing. He moves my legs down, so that they're both between his.

"Try this, babe. You'll love it."

With my legs together, somehow it just seems to put him in the right position so that he's rubbing against me in just the right place... within only a couple of minutes I'm stiffening and gasping from his persistent strokes, and hearing how turned on I am brings him to the point of release seconds later, before his whole body loses its tension and he rests his head on my shoulder, breathless.

We're actually silent for a few minutes afterwards. Even after he's removed himself, we lie tangled up in each other. As I look up at him, neither of us needs to say a word. That was one of the most incredible orgasms I've ever had.

When we're lying in bed side by side again, I think it's safe enough to voice my worries.

"I couldn't be happier for you, Alex. Today's been the best news ever – but what's it going to mean for us? How are we still going to see each other when you're living in London?"

He's silent for nearly a minute before he answers.

"Wish I knew, babe. It's not going to be easy. I can't even say I'll come home every weekend. They can film really long hours, seven days a week. All I can tell you for certain is this: I won't forget about you."

Why doesn't that sound good? It's a bit like, 'I'll never forget my first love', the kind of thing old people say when it's years later and they're married to someone else.

"I won't forget about you either, Alex. I just don't know how I'm going to cope with missing you so much. I'd try getting a big bottle of your aftershave to sniff on when you're not there, but last time I did that, I just got horny, jumped in a taxi and offered to fuck your brains out, if you remember."

He laughs.

"Oh, I certainly haven't forgotten that... soon as we get up, I'm going to Google two things: the price of the biggest bottle of my aftershave and train tickets," he looks at me, with raised eyebrows and widened eyes, then says in a comically deep voice, "for when you get the urge."

"Don't joke about it. I'm worried."

He lifts himself up onto an elbow, so that he's facing me. "Zo, if we start getting in a panic about it, we really will end up breaking up, 'cause we'll drive each other mad worrying about it. Let's just enjoy the time we've got left, then just see how often we can get together. Just remember: I love you. They could pick me up and put me down on the moon, and that wouldn't change."

"I love you too, Alex," I answer, snuggling into him for a last cuddle before we head back downstairs.

I just hope we can make this work.

CHAPTER 24

"So, this wonderful boyfriend who'd never leave you is... leaving?"

I'm in Café Italia again with Dad. I decided not to bring Alex along in the end. If he's going away in a month or so, it's probably not really that vital that they meet. Not yet, anyway.

I shoot him an angry look.

"At least he's telling me beforehand, which is more than you did. Look, Dad, I thought we'd agreed to try to move on. That won't happen if you keep criticising my boyfriend."

"I know, love, and you can tell me I've got no right to be annoyed all you like, but I'm still your father, whether I disappeared for ten years or not. I just don't want this boy to hurt you or mess you around. If he's going to be moving away, perhaps it might be best if you finish it with him."

I hear Dad's words, but they make no sense to me whatsoever. I've been in love with Alex since the minute I met him. I spent a whole year hovering around him in awe, before I could really be with him. Then when we finally did get together, he's turned out to be the sweetest, most fun, sexy, caring, just... everything boyfriend I could ever want. It's like meeting him is payback for all the boyfriends I've missed out on: I got all the best bits in one person. So after waiting so long, I'm supposed to dump him?

"There's no way I could ever finish with him, Dad," I say, fiddling with a spoon. It may not last forever, but if it does end there's no way I could cope with thinking it was my fault.

He puts his arm around me and gives me a shaky cuddle.

"Well look, love. I guess it's going to be a long time until I can accept this boy, and if I remember anything about how I felt about your grandad when I was first seeing your mum, I bet he doesn't like me much either,"

It's true, I think. Parents have got some sort of Radar, one which obviously keeps working even if they go away for a decade.

"but I can't stop you, can I? Just don't let this boy break your heart, but if he does... well, I'll be here."

I actually lean into him a bit. It's not the first hug we've had in our recent meetings, but it's the first one that contained any real feeling on my part.

"Thanks, Dad."

I never thought I'd say this, but I'm actually glad he came back into my life. I'm still a bit angry with him for not being around for the last ten years, but maybe I've got a future with two parents ahead of me now.

In the three weeks before Alex has to go, we spend as much time as we can with each other, doing all the things we've loved doing since we got together; we go for a meal at Le Bistro again and because we're both over eighteen and think we're sophisticated adults now, we order a bottle of red wine and pretend to like it. He wins another Minion from the arcade machine at the beach, so we've got one each now. He promises to take his with him. And of course, we spend loads of nights at our homes, either curled up together on the couch watching a film, or just talking.

The only trouble is, it's different now. We used to be able to do these things just for enjoying each other's company; it was just about being together. Now there's the unspoken premise that everything we do is about being together *while we can,* which can kind of spoil the mood if we allow ourselves to stop and think about it.

We combat this the mature, sensible, adult way: by just not thinking about it.

When I'm not with him, I'm busy going to extra study sessions and revising. My exams start in a couple of weeks, more or less the time he goes away. I'm just hoping I can take the 'immerse myself in my work' approach and not the 'fall apart completely' one. It's not just Alex who doesn't want to still be in Sixth Form next year.

One lunchtime, Jay tells me he's got an idea. He says he's spoken to his parents, and they've agreed to him holding a bit of a send-off party for Alex at their house. Not as big as his 18th, and obviously some people who were there at that party certainly won't be invited to this one. It'd just be us, and some of Alex's mates.

"I just thought, since he left so suddenly, no-one really got a chance to say goodbye. And he

did kind of get into the argument with Burton
trying to stick up for me as well as you. Mum
said we could use the pool area and patio.
Pool party!", he says, affecting a ridiculous
American accent. After all, it's all a bit high
school movie, not something you do too often
when you live in a North of England suburb.

I smile at Jay, knowing what he's really
thinking.

"You just want to get a look at my boyfriend in
his pants, don't you? All dripping wet as he
climbs out of the pool."

I know Jay fancied Alex before I was with him.
Before he met Connor, he told me he tried
approaching him to see which side he played
for. Not Jay's, unluckily for him. Still, I don't
blame him and anyway, soon I guess I'll have
to get used to half the country having a crush
on my man.

Jay tries to look innocent. And fails miserably.

"That hadn't crossed my mind, but now you
mention it, I suppose it could be interesting. I
just thought it'd be nice if we could use the
pool. It should be warm by the end of June
and it won't get dark 'til late, so we could sit
out on the patio."

It is a lovely gesture, and let's face it, one no-one else could make. Their pool is huge and even their patio's the size of a tennis court. It'd be a great way to give Alex a night to remember before he leaves. I reach across and hug Jay.

"Thanks, Jay. If you're sure, that'd be lovely. Tell your mum I'll sort everything out and make sure there's no mess afterwards."

Jay comes closer to me, smiling.

"Two words, Zo. Caterers and cleaners."

As I've said before, most of the time I forget Jay's minted.

"That's so kind of you, Jay. Please, thank your parents for me. I'm surprised they're willing to do it, considering. It's pretty great of them to host a party for," I roll my eyes upward as I try to find the exact words, "the boyfriend of the girl who isn't going out with their son when they always thought she was."

"Well, they didn't really think that, did they?" he replies. "Maybe they see you as the girl who's always been there for their son. Maybe they know this is going to be a tough time for you. I know I do," he tells me, giving me another friendly hug.

A little tear starts up in my eye, but I wipe it

away quickly.

"Thanks so much, Jay. You're a brilliant friend."

Wow. Pool party it is, then. Better dig out my bikini and do my legs.

CHAPTER 25

When I get home, I have to park on the road because there's a car on the drive. Steve's car. Bit early for a date, I think, before noticing that Mum's car isn't there.

I enter and call, "Mum? You here?"

Everything looks normal in the hallway, but when I turn into the living room, it's a different story.

We've been burgled and, just to add insult to injury, they seem to have been intent not just on nicking stuff, but on causing as much chaos and damage as possible. In the corner of the room is a gorgeous old glass display cabinet that used to be my great-gran's. Mum collects those coloured paperweights, the ones that look like crystal balls (in fact, I used to play with them as a kid, pretending to tell fortunes) and she keeps them in there. Or rather, she used to. Now, the wooden frame of the cabinet's intact, but every pane of glass is smashed or cracked, and the paperweights themselves have been lobbed around the room like tennis balls. It looks like one of them's knocked the mirror off the wall, whereas another one's broken the vase Mum kept on the window sill.

Looking around, I can see some other stuff missing. Mum had two bronze models of dogs on the mantelpiece. She loved them, and now some thieving bastard's probably flogging them for buttons. A photo of me when I was about five, first year of school maybe, has been taken as well, probably because it was in a silver frame. I don't even want to look upstairs to see what they might have messed with up there.

During the seconds that I've been looking around taking everything in, Steve appears through the back door.

"Alright, Zoe. I guess you can see what's happened. Looks like it was just kids, they've only taken things you can carry. They've had all the drawers and cupboards open to see if there was any cash lying round, and your Mum's laptop's gone."

Oh great, that probably means I'll see my laptop's gone when I go upstairs. At least we don't leave much money in the house. I ask Steve how he got in, and where Mum is.

"I called round about an hour ago. I knew Gem wouldn't be in, but I wanted to pop some seeds she's wanted to try through the letterbox."

One of the things Mum and Steve have in common is a love of gardening. It's the dullest thing in the world, but it keeps them happy I suppose. They're always swapping off-cuts and seedlings from each other's gardens. And I get to wind Mum up about him coming round to tend to her clematis...

"I heard noise in the house, and like I said, I knew it wouldn't be her, and I could see your car wasn't there, so I knocked and called through the letterbox. That must have made them run off. I went round the back and found the door had been forced. After that, I thought Gem wouldn't mind if I let myself in. I called her up immediately and told her about it, but there's been a family of four brought in with serious injuries after a crash on the motorway, so she can't get out of work for two more hours. I offered to fix a new lock on the back, so here I am."

I walk through the house, into our small garden and out towards the alleys that run behind my road. There are two of Mum's paperweights on the ground. One is smashed beyond rescue, but the other just has a crack in it. Maybe it won't look too bad with a good polish. A few feet down the alley, the photo of me is lying on the floor. They obviously weren't interested in that, just the frame. Good. I know Mum would have a backup copy of the picture somewhere, but it might have been on her laptop for all I know. It's crumpled and there's a rip in one of the corners, but I should be able to fix it.

I go to start tidying up, but Steve tells me I should leave everything where it is until the police have been round. The kitchen's not too messy, so I reckon it'll at least be okay to put the kettle on.

Once the new lock's on the back door, we sit and have a coffee. After about half an hour, I assure him I'll be fine if he needs to get going, but he refuses to leave me. In fact, he stays around all evening after Mum gets back, insisting that he won't leave her alone. I don't feel too bad about going round to see Alex as I'd planned before this happened. Mum's always been pretty tough, and if she isn't feeling that way tonight, she's in safe hands.

'X Y, Z'

CHAPTER 26

The pool party's scheduled for 24th June. I'll have finished my exams, and it'll be Alex's second to last weekend before he leaves to start his new job. Normally, I'd look forward to the idea of lying on a patio or lazing by the pool, drinking and having fun with my mates, but I'm dreading this day coming round, because it's another day closer to when he really will be leaving me.

We're just not talking about it anymore. We're spending all the time together that we can manage, but we're not discussing how either of us feel about having to be apart. Probably because we both know how the other one feels.

"What do you think, then?"

I've finally decided on a dress for the prom, and I'm modelling it for Alex in my room. I've gone for a change from my usual favourite colours and chosen a cream silk dress, with a pattern of smudgy, painted lilac flowers around the bottom of the skirt in a circle.

"It's lovely, babe, but to be honest I wouldn't have bothered buying a new one. Your black and red one's the best; you always look gorgeous in that."

Not buy a new dress for the prom? Boys just don't get it, do they?

"Well, maybe if you were going to be there I'd have worn it," I smile, "but at least now you can sit at home thinking you've done better than any of us, without even having to do the exams."

His face falls, and I see him clenching his teeth. What's he going to say?

"Actually, babe, by the time your prom comes around, I won't be sitting at home. They've brought my start date forward a week. I'll be sitting in whatever house they put me in, learning my first set of lines."

I'm turning away from him, so he can't see the look on my face. So I've got a week less with him than I thought. I was looking forward to spending the night with him after the prom, or going on a few last dates together. Now every minute seems to be ebbing away, faster and faster.

I've slipped my dress off now and returned it to its hanger. I sit next to him on my bed and cuddle into him. He puts his arm round me and sighs.

"I know, Zo. I've been dreading telling you. We've just got to be strong. Do you love me?"

"You know I do," I say, a little surprised he could even ask.

"The we're going to be fine, because I love you too and as long as we've got that, nothing else can break us up." He gives me a kiss, before obviously thinking he should change the subject.

"Anyway, any chance of a sneak preview of your bikini before this party then? "

When we get to Jay's house on the evening of the party, Ron and Ang are sitting in their front room. It's a huge room which looks almost empty, despite the huge cream leather corner sofa and telly the size of Birmingham.

In the centre of the room there's one of those coffee tables: a glass top, with a statue of a dolphin holding it up instead of legs. When it happened, Jay told me that when you win the lottery, they send someone round to your house to give you advice on how to cope with your overnight millionaire status. I wonder if they brainwash everyone into buying those coffee tables as well?

"Go through to the back, Zoe love," they say casually. "And is this Alex? We haven't seen you since Jason's birthday, but we've heard a lot about you."

Alex looks a little alarmed. I guess he's thinking of how Ron and Ang always thought Jay and I would get together.

"Mr and Mrs Williams, can I just say, thank you so for much for doing this. I mean, it's not like you even know me really."

Ron looks at him and smiles.

"Any friend of Zoe's and all that," he says, "especially since Jason told us how you ended up leaving school through standing up for him."

We go through to the back of the house, where Jay's sorting out the music and Connor's arranging drinks in the fridge. They're both still fully dressed.

"Hi Zo, Alex," he says, leaving the music to play. "No-one else is here yet. Go and get your cozzies on and get a drink."

Next to the pool, there's a small changing area. It feels a bit weird, actually. Obviously, I've seen Alex's body a hundred times, but we've never done something like go swimming before. I don't even know if he can swim, I've never asked. Still, it's not like we're going to be doing lengths or anything, is it? I've never really been to a pool party. I've been here to swim with Jay a few times over the years, but this is the first party he's held at the pool. What do you do? Just sit round drinking and hop in for a paddle every now and then?

"Ready to go, then?" Alex asks, twanging the back of my bikini before swinging me round to face him and looking down at my boobs. "I've got quite a good breast stroke if you're interested."

I know I joked about it, but I think he actually could get a hard on at a funeral... not that I'm complaining.

"Later," I tell him, as we walk out to the pool area. "Let's get a drink."

The rest of the evening is great. We all get a

bit drunk, but not too much, and divide our time between messing around in the pool and sitting on loungers on the patio enjoying the late sunset, eating burgers and a cake shaped like the 'Croft Estate' sign that appears in the show's opening titles, only this one's got 'Goodbye and Good Luck, Alex' iced onto it as well.

Alex and I are sharing a lounger. We're both still in our damp swimwear, so we've got a blanket over us to keep us from getting cold. Everyone else has gone into the house, probably to give us a bit of time alone. His mates have all said tonight how much they'll miss him and have been pestering him for Kellie Ashton's number all night once he let slip that he's got it, but it's as though everyone knows I'm the one this is going to affect most.

After a few minutes of kissing, while we're tangled up in each other beneath the blanket, he says, "Babe, after the one where I got with you this has been one of the best parties ever. I'm going to remember this forever. Thank you."

"Don't thank me, thank Ron and Ang. Or Jay for thinking of it."

"I'm thanking you because it's only good

because of you. In fact, I only care about the 'Croft Estate' role because of you."

Not sure how you work that out, I think to myself. The thought of you going is killing me, and anyway, it's not as though I inspired him to get into acting, is it? So I ask him what he means.

"You make me want to be a success. If I hadn't met you, I'd probably still be happy enough doing the chorus of the local panto. Now I'm determined to make enough money so I can look after you... and maybe help you move to London?"

I'm shocked. He knows I'm planning to go to Manchester. What does he expect me to do, give up on my degree plans? I can't say anything in return, just, "But..."

He pulls the blanket round us a little tighter.

"I know, you've got Manchester. And trust me Zo, I know it's important for you to get your degree. I just can't bear the thought of being without you. I'd be making enough money for us both, just about. Would you, I mean, could you think about transferring to a degree course in London? I mean, you're going to do English, surely you can find a place for that down there?"

I still don't know what to say. Part of me feels annoyed. If he wants to be with me that much, why doesn't he come with me to Manchester? Why should it be me who has to change my life to fit in with his plans?

The other part of me understands completely. He can't help the fact that most TV work, if that's the direction his career's going to go, is based down South, and it's not as though I'm aiming to do some niche degree that you could only find at one particular university.

Still, as I've already considered, it's too late to change courses for this September. Maybe I could transfer to London after my first year. I've heard you can do that, change courses and start at Second Year level somewhere else. I promise him I'll think about it.

It won't change the fact we'll have to manage for a whole year apart, though.

CHAPTER 27

It's been a week since he left.

Of course, I cried like a baby for the first twenty-four hours after I said goodbye to him on his parents' driveway as he got into the car to leave, but I've been surprisingly calm since.

I'm not lounging round the house crying all the time. It's not as though I haven't known this was coming, and it's not as though he's dumped me either. We're going to stay in touch. He called me the day after he got there. He's staying in a four bedroom house, with two other actors from the show. They're both a bit older than him, twenty-two and twenty. He said they seem nice enough, but he was struggling with having to cook for himself. And that he was missing me.

I'm okay through the day. It's the evenings that are difficult. That's the time when I'd have gone round to see him, or he'd have come round to me and we'd watch a film, talk about how our days had been... and almost always, end up in bed together. I think that's what I miss most. I'm not some sex-mad slag; I just miss the closeness, the knowledge that this was something we couldn't, wouldn't do with anyone else. It was something for just him and me.

Still, tonight I've got the prom to take my mind off being without him. I'd have loved for Alex to have stayed in school until the end so I could spend the night dancing with him, but I'm going to have just as much fun with Kate and Jay. Danny and Connor don't go to our school and you can't bring guests, so it's just the three of us together. It'll be great. Just drinking and dancing, with no men complicating things.

We all get ready separately at our homes, then get a taxi to pick the three of us up in turn. When we arrive, we stride into the venue, the function room of a local hotel, three abreast. Mr Burton is there, taking peoples' tickets at the door in a tuxedo which he obviously keeps for the Sixth Form ball and probably no other occasion.

275

When we walk through to the bar, Miss Dey is sipping a glass of wine. She doesn't look too bad when she dresses up, actually. It's kind of weird to see her in a strapless dress, drinking alcohol. I don't know why, but I don't tend to think of teachers as being human, but I suppose some of them must be.

We spend about an hour or so chatting and having a drink. It's strange to think that the only other time I'll see a lot of these people ever again is when the exam results come out. After that we'll all go our separate ways. Not me, Kate and Jay though, of course. They're both aiming to do Science-based degrees, but we'll always stay in touch with each other.

Miss Dey asks me if I'm still in touch with Alex. Of course, she won't have seen anything of him since the day he left school in March. I tell her we're still together. She smiles.

"Zoe, I'm just glad you did get together in the end. To be honest, it was almost funny to watch. I'd see you, gawping across the room at him throughout Year 12, then you started edging closer by working with him. And I could see he didn't mind at all. But then... nothing. I was starting to think I'd have to shut the pair of you in a book cupboard until you finally worked it out."

I nearly spit out my wine.

"Miss! I can't believe you just said that!"

Also, maybe I can't believe it was so obvious I liked him - no, we liked each other- for that long, even to her.

"What? Just because I'm a teacher, I wouldn't understand? Anyway, I'm just glad you sorted it out. Is it true what I've heard that he's going to be in 'Croft Estate'?"

Everyone knows about it now. Once he'd signed the contracts, it kind of got out.

"Tell him I'm pleased for him. I'd have had him back in my class, but I don't think grovelling to Andrew was ever going to be Alex's style, was it?"

I guess Andrew is Burton's first name. I've seen 'Headteacher: Mr A. Burton, B Ed, NPQH' on the big sign outside the school and on letters, I'd just never cared much what it stood for. I'm also guessing Miss Dey doesn't really like him either, from the tone of her voice.

After a while, I need a pee. I grab my bag and head off down the corridor. When I enter the toilets, one of the cubicles is in use. I think nothing of it and go for the one furthest from it, at the other end of the row, nearest the wall.

Afterwards, I'm giving my hair a tidy-up and reapplying my lipstick, when I notice that no-one left the other cubicle while I was in mine, the door's still shut and no-one's come out since. Maybe they're one of those people who are dead squeamish about even being seen near a toilet, so they're waiting for me to go before they leave. Again, I think no more of it and am about to head back to the party, until I hear a groan come from inside the cubicle. I turn back and give a gentle knock on the door.

"Are you okay in there?"

A pair of feet rise up, as if they're trying to hide and make the cubicle look empty. I tell them it's obvious someone's in there and ask again if they're alright.

"I'm fine. Piss off, freak."

Sasha.

"Well, you know what? I was worried about you for a second there, but I'll leave you to it."

I have my hand on the door when she changes her mind.

"Wait... Zoe. Don't go."

I think that might be the first time she's ever

used my actual name without rhyming it with a sex act. What's going on?

"Okay, Sasha. What's wrong? Have you been sick? Are you too pissed to walk back to the room?"

"No," she snaps. "Look, I need two things. I left my bag in the room so I can't text any of my mates. You'll just have to do."

Oh wow. That makes me feel really keen to help her. Still, I'm not a bitch like her, so I stay.

"Don't suppose you've got any pads on you, have you? I've come on. And can you go back to the cloakroom and get my jacket?"

I don't have any pads, but I buy one from the machine and pass it under the door to her. I'm starting to wonder if I'm really pissed and hallucinating this whole thing. I'd never have imagined I'd be spending my Sixth Form prom helping out the girl who pretty much treated me like shit throughout the whole of my time at school. Okay, I've helped her out with her biggest problem, but I'm not her bloody slave.

"Why can't you get your own jacket? I don't see why I should go down there and get it for you."

I hear her sigh again, only this time it sounds a bit more pained and desperate.

"Because I'm really in pain here. And to be honest," she pauses, "Look, I'm going to open the door. I can't believe I'm doing this."

The door opens and I can see why she doesn't want to leave the toilet. There's a lot of blood. The skirt of her dress has quite a few stains on it, even at the front. Sasha looks terrible. I can see she's really in pretty bad pain. This is embarrassing for us both.

"Er, look, Sash,"

What? What did I just call her? Like she's a mate or something? I guess it just came out because the only other girl I've ever been a in a cubicle with, knickers round ankles, is Kate.

"Look, unless you've come out in a floor-length coat in July, I don't think any jacket you've got is going to cover this up. Maybe I should see if Reception have got a blanket they could lend you."

I go to leave, then she seems to get a stabbing pain through her body. She bends forwards and moans with pain. What's wrong with her?

"Sasha, have you always had such bad period pain?"

"No, never like this," she says quietly. The she laughs. "Actually, I guess I should be glad it showed up at last. It was a couple of weeks late. Not that I was worrying about being pregnant or anything."

Oh no, I think. You're not pregnant. Not anymore, anyway.

 I crouch down to her level and touch her shoulder.

"Sasha, I don't think this is just regular period pain." I pause before going on, "I think you actually have been pregnant and this is a miscarriage."

Her face is blank with disbelief.

"But, I can't be... couldn't have been." Her lip starts wobbling and tears are forming in her eyes.

God, this is weird beyond belief. I'm spending my Sixth Form prom in a toilet, helping Sasha McCormack understand she's lost a baby.

"Sash, unless you bleed like this every month, and you did say you were late... it really can't be anything else. Sorry."

I know she's a cow, but even I feel sorry for her right now. Her makeup's a mess, her dress is ruined and she's just had the biggest shock of her life.

I leave her for a couple of minutes to go and ask for a blanket, telling her not to answer the door if anyone else comes. I find a 'Cleaning in Progress' sign on a mop bucket in the corner and put it on the exterior door. Hopefully she'll be left alone until I come back.

As I'm heading back, carrying a thick tartan blanket, there are a few thoughts whirling round my head. What am I going to do with her? I was planning to have a few drinks tonight so I didn't come in my car. I guess I'll have to call a taxi and just see her home. Before I dig my phone out of my bag to call the cab, there's one other person I want to speak to.

"Mum? Can you talk for a minute?"

Mum's having a night in with Steve tonight while I'm out. I can hear her Adele album on in the background. Lucky old Steve, he's obviously in for a fun night. I just need to borrow Mum first.

I explain Sasha's bleeding and pain, which Mum concurs definitely sounds like an early miscarriage. She said at such an early stage she'd probably be okay if she just went home and stayed in bed for a day or two. With it being a Friday night, if she went to a walk-in centre she'd probably have to wait for ages only to be told what she already knows. There's nothing any doctor or nurse can do to stop it once it's started happening. Mum tells me to make sure I advise Sasha to see a doctor on Monday though.

I call the cab, and while we wait for it, Sasha wraps herself up and we head towards the entrance, going as quickly as we can past the function room in the hope that we won't be seen. I've already had a couple of 'Where r u?' texts from Kate.

Outside the hotel, she sits on a wooden bench, while I stand up, so I can see the cab coming and flag it down.

"I guess you'll need to tell your boyfriend, maybe when you've got your head round it yourself. Does he go to our school?"

She just responds with "Hmmm," before saying, "There's no way I should have got pregnant. He said he couldn't have kids."

I'd laugh if this wasn't so serious. She didn't really fall for that, did she? How many times have I seen that on 'Jeremy Kyle', when half the time the 'man' who supposedly couldn't have kids was about seventeen? How on earth do they know at that age? Sasha must have worked out what I'm thinking, because she snaps as me.

"Drew's different. He's not some kid from Sixth Form. He's got two kids already. He told me he'd had the op after that, so he was safe."

Drew? That's not a name you come across too often, sounds American. Or... it's short for Andrew. As in Andrew Burton.

Oh my God, Mr Burton!

Have Sasha and Burton been having an affair? She might be eighteen, but that's still well creepy. And what does she see in him? She's always been able to have any lad she wants at school, with one notable exception.

I lower my voice and move my face close to hers, so we couldn't be heard if anyone passed by.

"Do you mean Mr Burton? Have you been having sex with him?"

She doesn't say anything, but it's clear from her embarrassed, indignant face that it's true.

"Well you know what, Sasha, I guess that explains a lot. Why my Alex would have been expelled if he hadn't walked, but nothing happened to you."

At least she has the decency to look ashamed.

"I don't know why I went with Drew. I guess I'd had most of the other lads at school, so when he showed an interest in me – well, I thought it'd be nice to have a man, not just another boy."

"Sasha, a teacher who sleeps with a student, even if you are eighteen – that's not a man. That's a bastard. And a lying bastard if he said he couldn't have kids."

The taxi arrives. I put her in it, and even give her a hug. I relay my mum's advice about seeing the doctor in a couple of days. As I reach to shut the door, she stops me with her hand.

"Zoe... thanks for this. I wouldn't have blamed you if you'd told me to fuck off and left me."

"I wouldn't blame me, either, but I couldn't leave you like that. Look, forget about Drew," I say his name with heavy sarcasm," and find a proper man. Just keep your hands off my Alex."

I know. That was a bit unnecessary. I couldn't help it, though. Again, she looks a bit sheepish.

"Are you still with him, then? I heard he went to London."

"Well, he did, but we're going to still see each other," I tell her, hoping I sound more convincing than I feel.

The driver starts moaning, so I let her go and head back to find my mates. I might just say Alex called me and I went outside to chat to him. I don't think they need to know about this.

Still, for the rest of the night I'm in a bit of a daze. Sasha and Burton. I don't know whether to tell Alex or not. He'd be fuming. Was what he did illegal? I know she's eighteen, but he's still a teacher. That's got to be wrong. I guess it's up to Sasha what she wants to do. I might see how she is in a few days, and see how she feels about reporting him.

CHAPTER 28

It's been six weeks since Alex went to London.
I've coped; I've got my friends around me and I
meet up with Dad at least once a week now.
Mum's okay with it. I tell her he seems to have
changed, which she refuses to believe.
Understandable I guess.

I'm happy with the way things are, though.
Maybe he can't make up for the years he
missed, but I'm starting to feel I could count
on him to be there if I needed him now. I'm
even wondering about making contact with
Hope while she's off school for the Summer.
We may not have much in common except for
some shared DNA, but if you find out you
have a half-sister, it's impossible to not want
to meet her, isn't it?

I've been looking forward to this week for a

couple of reasons: first, if I've made it this far without cracking up, and Alex and I haven't broken up, it's a good sign we're going to last, and second, Alex will be making his first appearance on TV as a proper cast member of 'Croft Estate'! It gets much bigger audience figures than the local soap he was in last year. If he's popular (or unpopular, his character's meant to be a bit of a rebel and heartbreaker, but you know what I mean) with the viewers, this could be his really big break. I'm not normally a soap addict, but I'm going to be now. He told me the first episode he appears in is due to be screened this Thursday at 7.30, so Kate and Jay are coming round and we're all going to watch it together. How weird is it going to be, seeing his name on the titles of the country's most-watched soap? I feel so proud of him.

I really miss him, though. I know we talk on the phone a lot, as many days as we can, but I'd give anything to feel him holding me. And to say I miss his warm, sweet kisses and the promise of what they usually lead to is the understatement of the year... I've arranged to go and visit him in a couple of weeks. You have no idea how much I can't wait. I wasn't allowed to visit him at his house, before his episodes are screened, and in the first two weeks that his character's on screen, he's got quite a few TV and magazine interviews booked. Everyone's going to want a piece of him, and I feel a bit like I'm at the bottom of the list. Still, I know he hasn't forgotten me. Even on the days we can't talk, I always get a texted 'XY,Z', usually just before I go to bed each night.

The media buzz around the new family appearing on 'Croft Estate' is already starting. In our corner shop today, buying milk, I notice the TV guides on the shelves. On the cover of one of them, there's a small inset picture of Alex, and one of them has gone with him as the main cover picture, with the not-very original headline, "Bad Boy! Dylan Shocks Croft Estate!" Then there's another magazine with his face on the cover; a magazine supposedly aimed at girls my age, but bought by girls ages 12 to 14 called 'Babelicious'. I felt like 'Babelicious' told me everything I know about periods, boobs and boys about five years ago, although now I'm not sure it was right about everything. I mean, it certainly never warned me how grim that first blowjob would be, did it?

Needless to say, I buy them all and dash off home to look through them.

I flick through the two TV guides first. They're both fairly ordinary, giving a bit of description about the Taylor family and a few hints about what they might be up to in their opening storyline. The pictures that accompany them showed Alex in character as Dylan. He isn't wearing his pendant, they've put him in a jacket that really doesn't suit him, and they've brushed his hair up to make it look a bit spiky. Hmm. While I'm sure he's still going to win 'Sexiest Male' at the next Soap Awards, he looks better as himself. Oh well, I can always tell myself that while the rest of the world gets Dylan, I get Alex.

Then I look at the 'Babelicious' article. It's a double page, with a huge picture of him. This time he's not in character, at least I don't think so because his hair looks the way I remember it, but the clothes he's got on look new. The headline, in red letters, reads, "Sexy Alexei!!!" Turns out he has to use his proper name, there was already an Alex Ryan registered with Equity. Ha, that bastard Burton will always remember it now, along with the time Alexei Ryan told him he was a prick in front of a canteen full of his students.

After my eyes have taken in the latest pictures of him, I start reading the article.

*We catch up with new 'Croft Estate' bad boy (*Is that the only phrase anyone's ever going to use to describe him?) *Dylan Taylor, aka hot*

new actor Alexei Ryan to find out what it's like
to star in the UK's biggest soap, and if he's
looking for love...

Well, that doesn't alarm me too much, I think.
'Babelicious' know their target audience –
teenage girls who are desperate for their first
boyfriend, and usually still at the point of
fantasising that it could be their celeb crush.
Still, I can't help but think, no fantasising for
me; the viewers can drool all they like, but the
new star of 'Croft Estate' belongs to me.

I carry on reading the interview. I know I talk
to him often, but it's still not as often as I'd
like, and anyway, I'm enjoying the novelty of
seeing his words in print, in a national
magazine that I used to buy, because he didn't
just talk about making it big: he's actually
done it.

Q: So, Alexei. That's an unusual name. Is it
real?

A: Yes, it is. My mum's half Russian, so me and
my brother have Russian names. I don't mind
being called Alex though, just not Alexander!
(laughs)

Q: How did you get into acting?

A: I've always loved it. I wished my school still
did school plays, but they didn't. I joined a

drama club instead. Then I was really lucky because when I was in a panto with Kellie Ashton, she recommended me to the casting people on 'Croft Estate' and it all went from there.

Q: Wow! Lots of guys would like to be picked up by Kellie Ashton – do we detect a hint of romance there?

A: (laughs) Oh no, Kellie's a good mate, but that's all. Anyway, she's got Jamie (Benson, the Manchester United striker) - I'm not sure he'd be too happy if I moved in on his girlfriend! (laughs again).

What the hell is he saying? I know I was a bit jealous of her at first, but now I know Kellie Ashton really has just been a good friend to Alex. He's told me he's even been out for a drink with her, this Jamie the footy player and some of the other cast members. That's fine. But why is he even joking about the idea of 'moving in' on her? And more to the point, why on earth hasn't he mentioned the fact that he's got me, so he doesn't need Kellie Ashton?

If that wasn't bad enough, I can't believe what he says next:

Q: So is there anyone special in your life at the moment?

A: Well, since I moved down to London six weeks ago to start filming, it's just been so busy, so I've had no time for going out and meeting people. I think my biggest relationship's been with the pizza delivery guy – I'm struggling to cook for myself!

I put down the page in disbelief. I know he's been busy, but why hasn't he mentioned me? Why hasn't he said he's got a girlfriend back home that he's been with for almost a year? Why is he talking about going out and meeting people?

I feel sick. It's happened. The thing I was afraid of. Now he's getting some media attention, it's going to his head and pretty soon he won't even remember who I am. Then I look more closely at the photo. His face looks the same, as does his hair. The new clothes don't surprise me too much, I guess if I was earning the money he is, I'd do some shopping as well.

It's the pendant. He isn't wearing it. I know he has to take it off when he's in character, but he's not in character in this picture. Could he really forget about everything we had so easily?

I can't read any more. I put the magazine
down on the coffee table and sit back,
astounded. I feel a cold, numb sensation in
my stomach and I can feel tears welling up in
my eyes. He must have known I'd read that
interview, even if it is in a magazine I wouldn't
normally buy. If he wanted to finish with me,
couldn't he have done it before he left, or even
over the phone? That wouldn't have been nice,
but at least it would have meant he'd had the
guts to tell me himself, rather than leaving me
to read that he'd be meeting new people if only
he had the time, and not wearing the pendant
he promised me he'd always wear.

After a few, well, quite a few if I'm honest,
minutes of screaming and trying not to
completely go to pieces, I take a few deep
breaths and try to be a bit more rational about
it. I'm not stupid, after all. Even as a thirteen
year old 'Babelicious' reader, I knew the score.
There have been loads of cases of singers and
actors who've been told to avoid mentioning
their partners in the media, because they
might lose popularity if they don't appear to be
single and available to their fantasising
teenage fans... that's what it is. I bet there was
some adviser from 'Croft Estate' sitting next to
him as he gave the interview, telling the
journalist to leave out anything he might have

said about me.

What about the pendant, though? It's not like it's a wedding ring or something. Nobody else would know about its significance. Why wasn't he wearing that?

In the end, I decide I should at least see what he has to say about it. I know he's probably busy right now, because his phone often goes straight to voicemail throughout the day. As soon as I get the tone, I recite my rehearsed message, as calmly as I can: "Hey Alex, just saw your interview in 'Babelicious'. Give me a call tonight. Love you, bye."

That'll do. I won't say anything about the fact he hasn't mentioned me, or the pendant. Let's see what he says first. I'll just wait for him to get back to me tonight.

CHAPTER 29

Okay, how long should I wait before I get seriously worried? He's never left it longer than a night without calling or texting me, but it's Friday now and I left my message for him at Tuesday lunchtime.

Come on. There's got to be some explanation for this. Maybe he's just really busy. Maybe he's dropped his phone down the toilet. Phones are always breaking. Kate's always struggling to read her messages because the screen of her phone shattered so badly when she dropped it that it looks like a spider's web, and she can't get a new one 'til Christmas. Yeah, it'll be something like that.

I'm not convincing myself though. Between phones and social media, there's not really any excuse not to stay in touch with someone

these days. Unless, of course, you just don't
want to.

I've managed not to feel too worried or upset
for the last few days, but today I'm starting to
feel like it's time I got the message: he's
phasing me out of his life. Maybe he's not
going to dump me, but he's just going to be
busier and busier, less and less contactable.
He's probably even hoping I'll get fed up of
waiting and dump him because it'll be easier.
For him, anyway.

I feel like my heart's been ripped out. Alex
Ryan has been the centre of my world for
nearly two years: first, when he was the object
of my unspoken infatuation, and for the last
year, when I've never stopped pinching myself
to check that it was true; someone as
incredible as him was with someone like me.

He's been my first love. My only love. There's
no way I'll ever be able to feel like this about
anyone again. I know I sounded a bit crazy at
times (Kate used to tell me) when I'd talk
about our future together, but I never thought
for one minute that my future could involve
anyone but him.

Being without him for the last six weeks has
been painful, but it looks like it's something
I'll have to learn to live with. I'll be relegated to

being one of the fans, whose only access to him is tuning in to watch 'Croft Estate' four times a week. I'm starting to think it would have been better if he'd never spoken to me at Jay's party. Yes, I'd have missed out on the fun times we've had this year, the closeness we've shared and the love I've felt for him, and he said he felt for me – but at least I wouldn't have had my heart broken.

I wander up to bed. I take off my heart pendant and, instead of placing it on my bedside table, I put it away in my jewellery box. I don't want to see it when I wake up. Then, I push the seaside Minion off the bed and get in. When the covers are over my head, I allow myself to cry. Loud, physically painful sobs that feel like they're tearing me apart. My head hurts. My heart hurts even more; and the worst thing is, this pain will never leave me.

Mum knows I've been waiting for a call from Alex all week and how much it's getting me down, but she hasn't said anything about it. Knowing her tendency to be brutally honest, coupled with her reluctance to trust men (although Steve's lasted nearly six whole months now, he must be different), that's probably a good thing.

I look like shit the next day. My eyes are red

and swollen from all the crying, and I look like I've aged ten years overnight. Oh well, it's not like I'm ever going to have to worry about looking attractive again, is it? I had the fittest boy in the world and I lost him. Anyone else is just going to be a letdown - for them more than me, the state I'm in at the moment.

I spend the morning taking a long bath, full of bubbles. I lie there until my fingers go wrinkly and my head goes numb. Then I get dressed. I've arranged to meet Kate in town. She's decided I need a coffee and some retail therapy. Seeing as Kate's favourite form of retail therapy often involves knicker shops, I'm not sure how this is meant to make me feel better, but I know she's just trying to help. I can't see it taking my mind off things much though.

I'm almost ready to head into town to meet her, when there's a knock at the door. When I answer it, I'm surprised to see Sandra. Alex's mum. I invite her in, wondering what she's here for. If he's sent her to get the heart pendant back, or the bracelet, she can take them. I suppose she can even take the keyring he gave me the first day he said he loved me. I've always treasured it, but if he doesn't love me it's worthless.

"Hello, Zoe. It's been a while since Tom and I

have seen you. How are you doing?"

I suppose it is. Since Alex has been in London, there's been no reason for me to go round to his house. I wish I didn't look so rough.

"Hi, Sandra. Have you come with a message from Alex or something?"

Her face doesn't immediately drop, as if she's about to give me some bad news. In fact, she looks a little relieved.

"Err, no dear. In fact, I'd come to ask if you'd heard anything from him. His father and I haven't heard anything since last weekend. I understand he's busy and won't be calling every day, but I'm a bit concerned about not hearing from him for a whole week. Every time we try calling him it just goes to voicemail. I just thought I'd pop round and check. If you haven't heard anything either, maybe he's got a problem with contacting us."

Here's something you never thought I'd say: I could hug Alex's mum! Okay, no matter how nice she is to me I'll always find her a teeny bit scary (I blame the makeup), but right now she's given me a little bit of hope. If his parents haven't heard from him, maybe there is some rational explanation for him not calling me.

I tell her about how I hadn't heard from him since Monday, and that I was afraid he'd lost interest. Sandra seems surprised.

"I don't think you've got anything to worry about there, Zoe. When he has rung us, he always says he's just been speaking to you before, or will be speaking to you after, and a lot of his conversations with us involve him saying how much he misses you. If he's changed his mind about being with you, he certainly hasn't given us that impression."

"What about this, though, Sandra?" I open the copy of 'Babelicious' to the page with him on it. "He always said he'd never take his Russian letter pendant off, but he's not wearing it here. This isn't a photo of Dylan, this is Alex."

"Hmm, I don't know, you know," she says, squinting at the picture. "We bought this one as well. I'm going to keep a scrapbook of all the newspaper articles I can find on him. Are you sure it's not him as Dylan? I don't recognise those clothes."

I can't hide the disappointment from my voice. "No, I think they are his clothes. Look at his hair. It isn't styled the way it is when he's in character. He probably got some new things while he's been down there."

Sandra keeps trying to reassure me.

Eventually, I tune out what she's saying and take another look at the interview I didn't finish reading on Tuesday. My eyes scroll down to a question near the bottom of the page.

Q: On 'Croft Estate', you get to work with some of the country's best known actors. How does it feel to be able to do that at such an early stage in your career?

A: It's an honour, really, I can't tell you how lucky I feel. During my first day on set, I couldn't believe I was getting the chance to work with these household names. Most actors my age are still on ABC, but I've been able to jump straight to XYZ. I want to be at the XYZ stage as long as I can!

Does that mean what I think it means? Maybe he was trying to give me a message, something he knew only I'd understand.

I feel relief wash over me like a cool shower. I should never have doubted him. God knows what's happened: broken phone, broken pendant... I don't care, as long as we haven't broken up.

I remember I have to go and meet Kate. I write my number down for Sandra. We're assuming his phone has been broken. When he gets another he might not know my mobile number off by heart, but he'll know his parents' landline. Things are looking up.

When I meet Kate, I'm feeling better. We stick to coffee (she said she was going to try taking me to get hammered if I was still miserable) and I tell her about how Alex's parents haven't heard from him either.

"Problem solved, Zo", she says. "He'll probably call you up tomorrow, maybe on a new phone number. Honestly, all that whinging out of you for nothing," she adds, giving me a friendly shove.

I have to admit, I do feel more relieved. We spend the rest of the afternoon nosing round the shops, doing our usual thing of trying on stuff we wish we could afford in the designer concessions at Debenhams and the boutiques in the arcade, then going to Forever 21 or Primark and buying something more within our price range. I decide to spoil myself a bit today though. With my trip to London coming up, I want to look my best when I get to see Alex. It'll be the first time in almost two months, so I want to knock him dead.

I pick out another (seriously, I'm becoming as bad as Kate) matching underwear set and a really nice pair of shoes. I thought if we get to go out anywhere when I'm down there, I'll just wear his favourite black and red dress. For the daytime I'll probably just wear jeans, so I use some money Dad's given me to buy a couple of nice tops so I can compete with the girls in London.

Ha. I don't need to compete. My clothes mightn't be the most expensive, but as long as I get to drop them on soap heartthrob Alexei Ryan's bedroom floor, who cares?

Sure enough, on Saturday evening, I get a phone call from an unidentified number. Hoping it's what I think it is, I answer straight away.

"Zo, it's me."

I always love to hear his voice, but it's never sounded as good as it does now. He tells me how one of his housemates (who plays a really serious, geeky character in the soap) flushed his phone down the toilet when they were a bit drunk on Monday, and after realising that no amount of soaking in rice was going to rescue it, he's been and got a new one today.

"Mum said you thought I'd dumped you."

Oh thanks for that, Sandra, I think to myself. I was hoping to just style it out and pretend I knew all along there was something wrong with his phone.

"I didn't really," I lie. "I just missed hearing from you every day. I suppose I just panicked a bit. Hey, I read that interview you did for 'Babelicious'. You've hit the big time now, I used to read that! You'll have hundreds of screaming teenagers camped on your mum's doorstep now!"

I can almost feel him blushing down the phone line.

"That was a nightmare, babe!" he says, although he does giggle afterwards. "I'm trying to be taken seriously as an actor, and all they wanted to ask me was 'What's your favourite colour?' and 'If you were an animal, what would you be?' "

I think I've calmed down enough to ask him what I've wanted to know for days.

"How's your relationship with the pizza delivery man? Still the biggest one in your life? Or have you had time to go out and meet some other people?"

There's a silence at the other end. Not a very long one, but it's there all the same.

"Look, Zo, you know what it's like. I do want to meet some people down here. I can't sit in every night with Luke and Jack. But all I meant by that was that I want to make some new friends. Why would I look at anyone else when I've got you?"

Let me guess... because any girl you meet in London is actually there, while I'm miles away? I'm wary that anything I say will come out wrong, so I keep quiet. He goes on.

"It's alright here, but if I'm honest I'm living for the first chance I get to pop home to sleep in my own bed, have one of Mum's roast dinners... and be with you. They make you either lie about your girlfriend, or just not mention them. The other lads told me it happened with them."

Well, I have to admit I did suspect that was the case. I feel a bit stupid now.

"I hate the thought of you being lonely down there, missing home. I'm counting the days 'til I can visit you. Can I ask you one more thing, though? That photo in 'Babelicious', were you in character in that one, or is it you?"

I can hear him thumbing through a magazine. He's obviously got copies of everything he's been in as well.

"Err, that's me, babe. Do you like that shirt? I thought I'd go for a bit of a change with my first wages. I wasn't really sure about it at first, but I'm wearing it now, in fact."

It's no good. I have to ask him why he isn't wearing his pendant, if that's him. On his birthday, he promised he'd never take it off. However, since I got into a flap over nothing about his lack of phone calls, I'm ready for him to tell me the chain's broken or something. It's not that, though.

"I can't tell you that, babe. You'll find out when you come down. Anyway, got to go now. Remember, even if I don't call, I love you. Always."

I promise the same and end the call. What's he up to that he can't tell me?

A second later, I receive a text.

"XY, Z. Never forget that."

I send the same text back to him. I do feel reassured, that I can trust him and believe he won't go off with anyone else. I just wish we weren't apart. Him being faithful's not much use if I never get to be with him, is it?

CHAPTER 30

This is possibly the biggest week of my life. It's mid-August. To the thousands of A Level students all over the country, this means only one thing: results day.

Every year they show someone on the telly, usually some old fart who did their exams years ago with a quill, saying the exams are getting easier. I've don't know about that. Even though I've always had a calm, business-like approach to my studies, I still found them hard enough. Or maybe it was having to sit them with the thought of my boyfriend's impending departure hanging over my head that made things so difficult.

I just hope I haven't totally messed them up. The last thing I want is to be stuck in Sixth Form for another year. Every year we have a few of them – Year 14s they're called, just to make them stick out like sore thumbs a bit more – and I always felt sorry for them while I was in Year 13. I used to look at them, sitting at the edge of the common room where only a year ago they probably felt they belonged, wishing they were at uni like their mates. I swore I wouldn't end up being one of them.

However, I have been thinking about something.

I know Mum'll go mad. Dad'll probably have something to say about it as well. There's no denying it feels like the right thing to do, though: I'm wondering about going to London. It was hard enough doing my A levels without him. I don't think I'll be able to stick three years of a degree, only getting to see him every couple of months when my term breaks or gaps in his filming schedule allow.

I reckon I probably won't have done all that well in my A levels, because I was feeling so down about Alex leaving, so maybe I can get into some college or uni in the London area through the clearing system. It doesn't have to be exactly where he lives. It'd be okay to travel across the city to see him, rather than halfway across the country as it is now.

On the day itself, I turn the telly on while I

make a coffee in the morning. The news is showing girls (why is it always girls?) jumping up and down as they open their envelopes, despite the fact it's only eight o'clock. Our school won't be open for the results until ten.

Kate, Jay and I have agreed to walk up together. I could drive, but I'm a bit wary of driving home if it's bad news, and we've also considered the idea of going to the pub across the road from school for a drink afterwards.

There's still over an hour 'til they're going to call for me, so I decide there's time for a soak in the bath. Mum heads out to work, wishing me luck and making me promise to call her as soon as I know, and I start to fill the bath up. I think today's a day for a Sweetie Candy bath bomb and extra Pink Paradise bubble bath. While I'm sitting there making myself smell like a human Dolly Mixture, I can think about the other thing I'm doing this week.

I'm going to London to see Alex this weekend! I can't wait. If I thought it was bad when I didn't get to see him much in the run-up to Christmas... well, I'm amazed I've survived, really.

Steve used to work in London. He's told me about a few places to go and see, apart from the obvious tourist landmarks. He even went as far as writing down some addresses and directions. I thanked him and put the piece of paper on the mantelpiece, but inwardly I was thinking, yeah right, like I'll be leaving Alex's bedroom for the whole weekend. All I can think about is feeling his body next to mine, one of his gorgeous kisses that I haven't had in weeks, and... well, you know the rest. Let's just say doughnuts have been off the menu for a while, but I'm looking forward to us both satisfying our hunger once we're back together.

Still, that's still 48 hours away. I've got to get through today and tomorrow first. It would be nice to sort a place in London out through clearing by Saturday, so I could surprise Alex with my news.

Not long after I've got dressed, I hear a beep outside the window. Jay's decided to drive there after all – well, he does live further away. I hop in and we set off, all three of us gabbling nervously about how this isn't a matter of life and death, and we'll all be fine even if we've all failed.

I know, I don't suppose we've convinced you either.

We get to school, and the first thing we see is a long queue. We thought we were getting there promptly, but maybe some people have been here since quite early. There are teachers and some of the school admin staff sitting at desks, sifting out envelopes and handing them to nervous-looking students.

It seems you have to join a queue according to your surname, so while Jay and I join the S-Z line, Kate leaves us to wait in the F-K section. Now all we can do is wait.

After what feels like about four years, but might have actually only been about fifteen minutes, we've all got our results. Kate's got the A and two Bs she hoped for, Jay's got two As and a C, which isn't as good as he thought he might get, but will still be enough to get him onto the course he applied for, and as for me...

I'm away from the noise of the hall, on a corridor, talking to Miss Dey.

"What would you do if you were me, Miss?"

"Well, Zoe, don't tell her I said this, but I'd stop worrying about what your mum thinks and just do it. I wouldn't normally support a student in dropping everything to be with a boyfriend, but I know Alex and I understand he's in a bit of a unique position. Like it or not, this job he's got probably pays more than you or I will ever make, and he can't exactly change the location. If you want to be with him, you're going to have to be the one who makes the move."

It's nice to hear someone lay out the muddle of thoughts I've had in my head in such simple, logical terms.

"Thanks, Miss. You've made it a lot clearer."

"There is one thing I don't agree with you on, though. Don't do clearing. You've just got three As, why on earth do you want to end up in a last-minute decision course in a place you don't know much about? If I were you, I'd take a year out, get any job you can get to give your brain a break and save up some money, then take your time to investigate courses in London that you want to apply for next year. With those grades, you'll probably get an unconditional offer."

I give her a hug and thank her for everything. She tells me to stay in touch and that she'd be happy to provide me with a reference when I apply for courses next year.

Yeah. I got three As. No big deal. I wasn't worried... much.

A year out, though? I can't imagine it. All I've ever really known is being at school, doing some form of studying. How would it work?

Would I stay up here, earn some money that I'd spend on train fares to London every few weeks? If I do that, I might as well have gone to Manchester. No. If I'm going to do a year out, I'm going to London to be with him.

The only way I could afford to be in London is if I lived with him – and let's be honest, if he paid for most things. He can afford to live there, I can't. He did say he'd be okay with that though, in fact I remember him saying it when we were talking at the pool party.

Mum'll go ballistic, and I'm not sure the idea of having to depend financially on Alex is something I can really live with.

But he's the one thing I can't live without.

I put the envelope containing my results in my bag and call Mum, then text Alex and Dad. I don't say anything to Mum about the idea of London yet. I think that's best done at home, maybe after I've got a couple of glasses of wine down her.

Heading back to the main hall to find my friends, I run into Sasha. I haven't seen her since the night of the prom. I have to admit, I didn't check up on her afterwards. It's not as though she's ever been my friend, is it? In the end I chickened out, thinking if she could be stupid enough to sleep with the head, that was her problem. I know he was in the wrong, but did she seriously think it would end well? That he'd leave his wife (although I admit, I don't even know if he has one; I know Sasha mentioned two kids, but he could be divorced) and shack up with a student less than half his age?

"Alright, Sasha."

She doesn't seem to have changed. Still too much makeup, brassy clothes and blonde hair which is a mixture of overcooked real thing and extensions.

"Alright, Zoe. What are your results like?"

This could be my chance to gloat. I know she won't have got three As. In fact, she's one of those girls who's fairly average academically, but has the sense to realise that and has chosen to get by on her looks. One thing I will give her, she is pretty. I don't know why she doesn't realise she'd actually look a lot better if she eased off on the slap and stopped frying her hair.

I'm not letting her into my plans before the people I actually care about, so I say, "Okay. I should be able to get onto the course I want. What about you?"

She glares at me, as though she doesn't want

to answer.

"One C and two Ds. Not exactly what I needed to get into Manchester."

The bitchy side of me wants to say I'm surprised she did as well as that, but I can see she's pissed off. And, no way, did she say Manchester? If I wasn't set on changing my course before, I am now. Imagine her showing up at my first lecture, or even worse, getting the room next to me at halls? I'd never be able to get any sleep for her headboard banging on the wall.

"Oh well, I'm sure you'll get something. You've always landed on your feet before." I look around to check no-one else can hear us. "What about the other thing? Are you okay?"

She assures me that she is, but when I ask her if she's planning to report Mr Burton, she becomes a bit evasive. I guess that means she's still sleeping with him. I decide not to question her any further and say goodbye. Hopefully I'll never see either of them again, anyway.

Through the school foyer's large plate glass windows, I see Kate standing by Jay's car, looking for me, so I give her a wave and start to make my way out towards the car park. Mr Burton is standing by the front door. He's wearing jeans and a casual shirt without a tie, as if he's desperate to show how real he is. A real prick. Alex was right.

As I walk out, he meets my gaze uneasily. I've got good results, and he'd usually congratulate a student on that... but I haven't forgotten about how Alex left, and neither has he. In the end, he comes out with a clumsy, "Well, erm, good work, Zoe."

I'm actually thinking to myself that right now would be a perfect time to pass on that message Alex asked me to give him a while back, but I am still going to want a reference from this school, good results or not. I smile at him and say, "See you round... Drew."

Just before I leave the building, I see his face freeze. I'm guessing only Sasha called him that, and he's just realised that if I know about him sleeping with her, he could be in some very deep shit indeed. I'm not going to report him though. That's Sasha's call, and it seems to me like she was a very willing participant. No, I think the fact that he'll be on edge about getting a phone call or a visit from the police every day for the rest of his career is a just punishment.

CHAPTER 31

The train journey seemed to take forever, but now I'm in a taxi, heading for the address Alex texted me this morning. I haven't said anything to him either about the idea of me coming down to London and us living together. I guess I have to talk to him before Mum, because what if it turns out he wasn't really serious and says no? Or he was serious then, but he's since decided he quite likes living with a couple of lads? I hope I'm not about to make a massive fool of myself. Maybe I should save the conversation for when I'm just about to get on the train home tomorrow night, otherwise it could mean a pretty awkward weekend.

The cab pulls up at a row of terraced houses, nice but not especially grand. This being London though, they're probably still worth more than Jay's parents' house, or maybe my entire road. If Alex makes it big, like film star, millions per movie big, we definitely have to move back up North. When he's that important we'll be able to live wherever we want.

My knock is answered within seconds. It's him. Actually him. He's sent me pictures on his phone and I've seen the ones in the magazines as well as watching him on telly, but he's here in front of me for the first time in almost eight weeks. As soon as the door is shut behind us, we throw our arms around each other in a desperate embrace, as if we're both determined to make up for the hugs we've missed in that time. And then we kiss.

I read somewhere once that if you don't have a drink for ages, when you do have one again, the tiniest sip of wine will go straight to your head. I've never tested that theory, but I'm here to tell you it's definitely true about kissing... the taste of his lips, the sensation of them pressed against mine in a series of short, quick teasing kisses before he pins me against the wall and explores my mouth with his tongue makes me almost delirious.

When we can finally pull apart from each other, he says, "Oh babe, I've missed you."

I just rest my head on his chest and say nothing. I'm just so happy to be with him again.

He takes my overnight bag and the tin of homemade biscuits his grandmother asked me to pass on to him, then gives me a tour of the house. Luke and Jack are out. He's given them express orders to at least give him the place to himsclf for the afternoon. Good.

It's a nice house: four bedrooms, so they have one each and the small box room is used for them to store suitcases and other junk. It's not too untidy, considering it's shared by three young men who probably don't see housework as a top priority. There is a sinkful of mugs and a pizza box in the kitchen, with about four slices left in it, though. Alex looks a bit embarrassed and admits the pizza's his. At least it doesn't seem to have had any effect on his body, which still looks pretty gorgeous to me.

"You'll have to get your Mum down here to give you a few cooking lessons," I tell him. I'm not ready to bring up the idea of me living with him yet, and even if we do get a place, I'm not sure the food situation would be any better with me in charge. Although, surely I can't be that bad. When your mum is out at work as many nights as mine, it's learn to cook at least a few meals or starve, basically.

"Mum, Dad and Leo are coming next week," he smiles. "Obviously, they can't stay here, they're going to find a Travelodge a few miles away. I'll have to do a proper tidy up before my Mum sees this place."

I could feel offended by the idea that he didn't think it was vital to clean the place up before I came, but I'm not. I haven't come here to see how tidy his room is. Speaking of which, we're at his bedroom door now.

He pushes at the door. "Well, are you ready to see where absolutely no magic happens at all?"

His room's okay. Obviously, as he was the last to join the house, he's got the third room at the back of the house, but it's still a decent size, with enough room for him to have a double bed. I recognise his duvet cover from his room back home and some of his belongings, but overall it feels odd and unfamiliar, as if we're about to do it in a stranger's house - but trust me, we're definitely about to do it. I'm not sure I can wait much longer.

He sits down on the bed, then flops back onto it, with his feet still on the floor. He raises himself up on his elbows and looks up at me.

"So, now you've seen everything."

"So I have," I reply, sitting next to him, then turning and leaning in for a kiss. Enough small talk. We both know what we want now.

After a couple of minutes of kissing, I feel what I've been missing for so long: his erection becoming more solid through his jeans. I consider sliding down and undressing him, but I don't want to wait. Instead, I stand up and start removing my own clothes, which he takes as a signal to stand up and do the same.

I suddenly feel a bit self-conscious. Not sure why. I mean, this is Alex, I've been with naked with him I don't know how many times, he knows me more intimately than anyone in the world; and yet I slip nervously under the duvet as quickly as I can, as if I'm afraid of him seeing my body. Maybe it's because we've been apart for such a long time, or maybe it's this room, which is neither of our homes really.

Either way, my nerves dissolve fairly quickly when he gets into the bed next to me and starts stroking my boobs. Reading my mind, he says, "Oh, it's been too long since we've done this."

I reach down to feel that he's totally aroused and ready for action. I move my hand up and down, causing him to murmur gently, "Oh babe, that's lovely. Keep going, please."

I keep stroking for a minute or two more, before turning away from him and lying on my side halfway down his body, so I can take him in my mouth. His slow, sexy breathing is an incredible turn-on for me. Knowing how much he loves it when I move my lips back and forth gently over the top of his penis makes me want to carry on for longer, but eventually he touches the back of my head, so I reposition myself next to him, where we can cuddle again at eye level.

"Zo, that was amazing. I didn't want to stop you, but I knew I'd have to if we're going to do anything else."

After an intense, passionate kiss he stares intently at me and says, "Your turn now."

I was hoping he'd say that. I've become a bit of a convert to some occasional masturbation while he's been away, but there's nothing in the world that can replace the feeling of his tongue, sending waves of pleasure through me and making me feel like the luckiest girl in the world.

Mmm. This is new. Instead of his usual measured, deliberate tongue strokes around the outside, he's being a bit more energetic. When he sticks his tongue up and down quickly I think I'm going to black out again, but I just about manage to stay conscious to enjoy every tantalising second of his attention.

When he finishes and comes back up to meet my eyes, I'm breathless. I have to admit, I'm wondering where he got that idea from. He never used to do it when we were together. I want to believe him when he tells me there's been nobody else while we've been apart, so where did he learn a trick like that?

He's hesitant for a while, but when he can see that I'm worried and thinking the worst about this, he admits the truth.

"Actually Zo, I read about it in that copy of 'Babelicious'. I've got to say, for a teenage girls' magazine, it's well rude."

I know. Why does he think I bought it every week when I was thirteen?

I have to laugh at the mental picture I have of him, sitting alone in this room, reading 'Babelicious' with its pink cover and free gift of a trial pack of Tampax. Still, that image is preferable to the thought of him not being alone. When I'm not there, anyway.

"I take it you liked it, then."

"I loved it, but you know what I want now," I

whisper to him, trying to sound as much like a sultry, breathy temptress as I can. Don't really think I'm pulling it off. I needn't worry though; he's eighteen and he hasn't had a shag in almost two months. I think I'm probably safe.

He warns me that after my previous efforts, he probably won't last very long, but I'm not much better. After only a few minutes of fast, deep thrusting we're both exhausted. Still, I look at his bedside clock and note that it's only two o'clock; he said his housemates wouldn't be back 'til around six. We've got hours to do it again, taking our time and enjoying each other's company.

On the other side of the room, I see my bag, with Steve's piece of paper outlining the attractions of London poking out. Sod that. I'm back next to the man I love. I'm going nowhere.

By half past five, we decide we'd better get up. If the other lads said they'd stay out 'til six, we'd better make sure we're out of bed and dressed. I know they'll know we've just been shagging all afternoon, but I don't want to make it totally obvious.

While I'm in the shower, Alex sits on the toilet with the seat down and talks to me while I

wash my hair. We start thinking about getting
something to eat, and he offers to take me to a
restaurant a few roads away which is a bit like
the one we used to go to back home. He tells
me it'll be okay; he's not so famous he's
unable to go anywhere, although he did say
he's learned not to be on the bus that goes
past the dance and drama holiday club, which
is run at a local high school, on his day off.

I agree, but make a mental note that for
tomorrow, I'll find the local shops, get the stuff
to make a roast dinner and cheer him up a
bit. Like I said, I'm no candidate for
'Masterchef', but I can bung a piece of meat in
an oven for two hours.

I get dressed in my red and black dress and
he puts on a lovely pale blue shirt with proper
trousers. He looks so gorgeous I could almost
forget dinner and take him back to bed now.
We come down from his bedroom after getting
ready, to Jack and Luke watching the telly.
Alex introduces us. They both look up and say
polite 'Hi's, before returning to watching
something with Ant and Dec in it.

I know I should be well used to the distinction
between actors and their characters, but it
still feels weird to be in a room with three
actors from 'Croft Estate' - especially when
two of them are people I only ever see in

character – and they're right in front of me, watching crappy TV shows and drinking beer. Jack, the one who plays a studious geek, seems especially strange to witness.

Dinner is lovely. I do hear a few whispers of, "Is that the new lad out of 'Croft Estate'?", although it's followed by, "No, don't think it is, look at his hair. Does look a bit like him though, doesn't he? Same eyes."

Alex orders a steak and I can see he's enjoying having some proper food for a change. Oh well, while I'm not offering to be some sort of servant when I move in, the way to a man's heart and all that... hopefully he'll still be up for the idea of getting a place with me.

We've finished eating and we're waiting for the bill, so I think now's as good a time as any.

"I've loved us being together again today, Alex," I tell him.

He reaches across the table to take my hand. "So have I, babe. It's been great. I think being busy has kept my mind off things a bit, but being with you again has made me realise how much I really have missed you."

"Do you remember what you asked me at the party at Jay's? Did you mean it?"

He stares at me. He knows what I'm talking about.

"Babe, are you saying you'd.."

"I want to come down here to be with you. The last eight weeks without you have been so hard and you were right: it's not as though I can't study English here, is it?"

He's struggling to get his words out. "Zo, it'd be, well, I'd love it..."

I take a deep breath before I go on. This is the bit I really don't want to do.

"There's one thing, though. We both know I couldn't afford to live down here. There's student halls and things, but if I'm going to do this, I want us to be together all the time. So it's not just having me round the corner like we did back home, and we'd meet up some days; I'm talking about living together, 24/7. And that'd mean you pretty much having to support me. Are you sure that's what you want? You can say no and I'll understand."

He takes a sip of his drink. Then, he stretches both of his hands across the table, taking mine and leaning over to look into my eyes.

"Do you want to know something, Zo? I haven't had much time off here, but when I have, I've been looking for flats. Looking for something I could afford for the two of us. If I found anything, I was going to ask you again. Sure, it'd be a bit tight, I'm not on Kellie's money, but if we went to one of the areas a bit further out, we could do it. All I wanted to know was whether you would. Guess I've got my answer to that question now."

He lifts my hand to his mouth and kisses it. This is it. We're going to live together.

I breathe a sigh of relief. That was the easy bit, though. Now I have to tell my parents.

CHAPTER 32

In the morning, I wake before him. It's kind of Sod's Law that if you're at someone else's house, you always wake before them and you have to lie there feeling awkward. After a while, I'm too thirsty and decide to go down and get a drink. I should be able to find my way round the kitchen, I think, or at least if I can't it doesn't bode well for my plans to cook later.

I slip on Alex's dressing gown and head downstairs. No-one else is awake, so I have a peaceful half hour, curled up on their couch, drinking coffee and contemplating what it'll be like when he and I do get our own place. It won't be as nice or as big as this, but it'll be ours.

At about half past eight, Luke stumbles down

the stairs. He's only got a pair of boxer shorts on, so he's a bit embarrassed when he spots me. Again, this is strange. As the soap's resident nice-but-dim hunky bartender (in fact his current storyline involves being the love interest for Kellie's character), he spends a lot of time with his top off.

I feel a bit awkward as well, so I mumble something about making Alex a drink and shoot back upstairs. Perhaps the noise of me coming up the stairs has woken him up, but Alex is sitting up in bed when I come back into his room. I put his coffee on his bedside table.

"Hi, babe. Just think, we'll be doing this every day soon."

The thought of it brings a massive smile to my face too. "I know, it's going to be great. I can't wait 'til we're living together."

I ask him for directions to the nearest shops, so I can get what I need for dinner. I haven't told him what I'm doing yet, I want to surprise him.

At the shops, I buy enough for Jack and Luke as well. I've no ideas what their plans are, but hopefully it'll be a nice 'thank you' for having some strange girl around, forcing them to cover up all weekend. However, judging by the prices in London, I can see Alex and I eating a lot of beans on toast when we get our own flat.

When I get back, he's still sitting up in bed, sipping another coffee. It's only ten o'clock and I don't think we've got anywhere to be, so I peel my clothes back off and get in with him.

"So, what's the plan for today?" I ask, as I cuddle into him.

He twists his head slightly and kisses me, a closed-mouth, coffee-scented kiss.

"Anything you like, as long as it ends with a shag." He starts to stroke my thigh under the duvet. "And begins with one as well."

I lie back, so we can do this properly. "I like your thinking, Mr Ryan," I smile, "although I do think there's some room for a shag in the middle that you haven't fully utilised."

He's lying down now as well, but not for long as he moves round so that he's above me, keeping himself off me using his knees, kissing and stroking me to make sure I'm completely ready for him.

I reach down and start stroking him. It's hard to imagine that this felt strange, even scary when I first met him. Now it feels like the most natural thing in the world.

We're both aware of the other two lads, who are both awake by now, so we know this has got to be a quiet one. He fishes a condom out of his bedside drawer, then guides himself inside me. It's an unspoken thing, but we go for one of our old favourites: on our sides, rocking each other gently, exchanging warm, heartfelt kisses in between whispers of, "This is so good," and "Oh God, babe, I love you."

Finally, he moves on top and we bring each other to a quiet finish: his breathing gets more and more intense and urgent, while I let out involuntary muted gasps of delight until I can't go on any longer.

After a while, we get up and make some breakfast, although it's actually closer to lunch time. Luke's gone out and Jack's girlfriend has come round, so they've disappeared up to his room. Alex and I are dressed, so we sit and eat our toast in the living room.

Although I'm worried about how my parents are going to take the idea of me going away, I'm happy. Things couldn't be going any better. I've got the A levels I wanted, Alex and I are solid despite us being apart, and we're going to live together.

I'm not sure I'm even bothered about it now,

but I ask him why he wasn't wearing his chain in the 'Babelicious' shoot if he wasn't in character. After all, he did say he'd tell me when I came to visit.

"Okay, babe. I was going to do this when you left, but I guess now's just as good."

He heads back to his room, returning with a small box. Don't worry, not so small it could only be a ring. Let's see how living together goes first.

"I got this for you. Before I knew you'd be coming down here, I wanted to give you something to make you think of me when we're apart."

Huh. Like that's necessary. But hey, a gift's a gift. I open the box.

It's two small white gold charms, each about the size of my little fingernail. The first is three letters, our special code, surrounded by a circle. The second is a tiny version of his Russian letter. I guess he had to leave it with them so they could copy the design.

"Oh, Alex," is all I can manage. I look up to see that wonky smile of his. He knows he's got it right.

"The XYZ was for your exam results, and the

letter was going to be for our first anniversary, but now I think you should have it to celebrate us getting a place together," he says. "We're going to have so many things to celebrate, Zo. It's going to be great."

In my head I'm thinking, let's just see if my Mum agrees with you.

I'll miss Jay and Kate too, but they're both headed to Liverpool on the same Science course, so we'd be going our separate ways anyway. And as for Dad, we may be getting on okay, but I don't think he can complain much about me moving away.

I give him a hug.

"Yeah. It's going to be perfect."

By around midday, we decide to go out. It's tempting to spend the whole afternoon in bed again, but we haven't got the place to ourselves the way we did yesterday, and anyway, it would be nice for us to do something together apart from that. To have the kind of afternoon we used to have before he came to live here.

We're too far away to be able to do any of the tourist attractions in an afternoon, and if I'm honest, I'm not too bothered about them. You see things like Buckingham Palace on the telly all the time; it's not going to look that much different in the flesh (or should that be in the bricks?), is it?

In the end, we just decide on going for a walk round his local area... although I guess it won't be his local area for long. After a few minutes of studying the window of an estate agents on the local high street, I can already see that when we do start flat-hunting, round here's going to be out of our price range. Still, we can have a wander around for now. I want to get to know as much as I can about his new world.

After about ten minutes walking, we come to a park. There are some people around, but it's fairly quiet for August. There's a kids' play area, which has got about five kids playing in it, and a few people throwing tennis balls for their dogs, using those things that look like ice cream scoops.

Alex and I walk on for another quarter of an hour or so, stopping eventually at a bench, where we sit down. We intertwine our arms and hold hands as I lean into him. I've missed this. I don't want to miss it again for too long.

As I sit with my head on his shoulder, a

thought enters my head.

"The only thing missing from this is a chocolate baton."

"Yeah, babe. Still, they weren't totally necessary , were they?"

I can sense he's looking down at me, so I turn my head up towards him, glancing at him for a second before we kiss. We hold the kiss for several seconds, almost as if we're afraid to let go of each other now we've found each other again.

Our romantic moment is suddenly interrupted by an interloper. If anyone was ever going to come between me and Alex, I used to fear it'd be Kellie Ashton or some other soap babe; I didn't think about a wedge being driven between us by an enormous, slobbering Great Dane... Alex and I are pushed apart as a pair of huge front paws plants muddy prints on my jeans.

A middle-aged woman comes scampering up behind.

"Oh, I am sorry," she says, a bit out of breath from running. "Beyonce! Bad girl! Get down now!"

Alex and I look at each other, trying to keep a

straight face. Beyonce? I've heard of people calling their dogs things like Dave or just Dog, but a Great Dane called Beyonce? I guess people really are different down South.

The woman obviously knows what we're thinking, because she says, "I know, it's bloody ridiculous, but that's what happens when you let your daughter choose a name. She hasn't frightened you, has she? I know she's a bit scary looking and heavy, but she's a big daft dollop really."

Alex reassures her that we're fine, it was just a bit of a surprise. Once Beyonce's calmed down a bit, we give her a bit of a stroke and she's soon plopping her slobbery jowls in my lap.

I can see that the woman is looking as closely as she can without it seeming rude at Alex.

"Don't mind me asking, love, but... are you Dylan Taylor?"

Alex blushes, but I can see he's actually dead pleased. You always hear actors saying they don't like being recognised and they just want to have privacy, but I bet when they were starting out, they all loved it really.

"Well, yeah. I play him. I'm Alex."

The woman puts her hand over her mouth in surprise. When she removes it, she remains fixed to the spot, looking at him in disbelief.

"I'm sorry to ask, but do you think I could get a photo with you? My daughter really likes you. She never used to watch 'Crofties' 'til she saw you on it, now she's hooked. She won't believe this. Wait 'til I tell her Beyonce's licked Dylan Taylor's face!"

Alex smiles. Looks like he can handle people getting his name wrong when it's because he's a soap star. He gets up from the bench.

"Sure, where do you want me to stand?" he asks, as the woman fumbles in her pocket and digs out a phone that's even older than my mum's. Because the phone's so old, it hasn't got a particularly good camera function and the first two pictures come out grainy and at bad angles, due to the fact that she has to press a button on the keypad, rather than just tapping the screen.

"Tell you what," Alex says to her, "pass your phone to my girlfriend and let her take it. She should be able to fit us both in better."

The phone is passed to me, I take the picture and the woman leaves, apologising once again for Beyonce, who by this point has bounded off across the grass and is in the process of depositing a massive turd on the football pitch...

I'm silent for a minute. Eventually, I look at him and say, "You just said I was your girlfriend."

"Well, yeah. You are," he says, with gentle sarcasm. "Surely you've noticed. Do you think I have sex twice in a day with the postman, or anyone who's passing?"

I give him a light dig in the arm.

"Funny. You know what I mean. You didn't pretend to be single, even though that woman's going to go home and tell her daughter, who's apparently your biggest fan, about this?"

He slides his hand into mine.

"If the PR people for the show want to alter my words when I'm interviewed for stuff like 'Babelicious' I can't stop them, but when I'm off-duty, there's no way I'm going to lie about you, babe. If they have a problem with that, they'll have to sack me, but we're going to live together and I'm not going to hide that from anyone. Anyway, I can see a café over there. Do you fancy getting an ice cream? I'll let you nibble my flake," he says, chuckling.

As we get up to leave, I point out, "Anyway, what are you on about? We haven't done it twice today."

He gives me that smile.

"Your train's not for another six hours, Zo."

I grab his hand and lead him in the opposite direction from the café. "Come on, let's go back."

Who needs a 99 in a strange caff when you've got a Calippo waiting at home?"

If there was even the tiniest bit of doubt in my mind about whether I'm doing the right thing, giving up everything I've ever known to be with him in this unfamiliar place, it's gone now: we're going to be fine.

I manage to cook the dinner without burning the house down. Okay, I got a packet of roast potatoes and used a can of mixed vegetables, but I reckoned that was alright because 1) Alex hasn't got many pans, 2) I didn't think he'd really mind; I know my roast potatoes are never going to be as good as Sandra's, so I was only ever aiming for passable and 3) Who wants to spend all day cooking? There's cheering your boyfriend up and there's completely wasting your Sunday.

Anyway, all three of the lads love it. As he takes the dishes to wash up, Jack even says, "You can definitely come again, Zoe."

Alex and I exchange nervous glances. Unless I'm happy with Alex picking somewhere for us to live without me being there, I might have to come down and stay a few more weekends while we find something together. If the other two appreciated me cooking for them, it should make them a bit more agreeable with the idea of that. Damn, I'm cursing myself for not having a go at doing proper roast potatoes now.

Alex is sitting at the table, looking at me, or at least he might be. He seems to be miles away. When I ask him what's on his mind, he replies, "Oh, just thinking about something my nan said one time. You know, Zo, that was great. You can really cook."

I have to get the eight o'clock train back that evening. He's got rehearsals starting early tomorrow morning, so if I waited until then, he wouldn't be able to see me off at the station.

Just before my train pulls into the platform, he makes me promise to text when I've got back safely, then says, "I can't wait 'til I'm not saying goodbye to you at the end of the day, because you'll always be with me."

Neither can I. This is the biggest thing I've ever done, but it's a complete no-brainer. No matter what Mum or Dad might say, I'm going to live with Alex. We share one last goodbye kiss before I board the train, but I'm not going home.

People always say home is where the heart is: if that's the case, then my home's with him. He's had my heart since our first night together. Alex Ryan isn't just my first love... I already know he's the love of my life.

Once my train's out of the station, I settle back in my seat and send him a text: 'I had a great weekend. I'll be home soon. X Y, Z.'

ABOUT THE AUTHOR

Insert author bio text here. Insert author bio text here